ALSO BY DEBL

D0888456

The Journ
Cracked Earth
Ash Fall
Crimson Skies
Raging Tide
Fault Line
Martial Law

EMPulse series
EMPulse
EMPulse2
EMPulse3

A Prepper's Cookbook: 20 Years of Cooking in the Woods

Time Shadows

Polar Storm

Look out for the thrilling sequel to *Shelter in Place:*
Dead in Winter is coming!

IS COMING

SHELTER IN PLACE

DEBORAH D. MOORE

PERMUTED
PRESS

A PERMUTED PRESS BOOK

ISBN: 978-1-68261-923-0
ISBN (eBook): 978-1-68261-924-7

Shelter in Place
© 2020 by Deborah D. Moore
All Rights Reserved

Cover art by KC Jones

PERMUTED
PRESS

Permuted Press, LLC
New York · Nashville
permutedpress.com

Published in the United States of America

"It is easier to stay out than get out."

– MARK TWAIN

CHAPTER ONE

August 3
Thursday

Rebecca Burns pulled her car into the long, tree-studded driveway. Her heart smiled at the lush green leafy canopy. There was never a time she felt more at home and at peace than when she was surrounded by trees and all the wildlife that came with them. She pressed the remote to open the attached garage and came to an abrupt stop when she saw her ex-husband's new car in her parking spot. He was behind in his child-support yet drove a new car while hers was already five years old and starting to need repairs she couldn't afford. She scowled and parked off to the side, giving him plenty of room to leave.

It had been ten years since Becca had returned home to care for the aging aunt who had raised her; five years since the blinders had been completely lifted and she saw her marriage in a new light, which wasn't always a good thing. Never being one to give up, she kept working at making the relationship better. The final straw came a year ago.

Leaving the groceries in the back of her SUV, she stomped through the garage, reached inside the open window of his luxury car, and yanked the garage remote off the soft gray leather visor. She tossed the remote onto the workbench and opened the inside door leading to the kitchen, slamming it shut behind her.

"What the hell are you doing here, David?" Becca asked the man sitting at her kitchen table. Her long, dark chestnut-colored hair framed her face and seemed to intensify the fury burning in her deep brown eyes. The anger that rolled off her five-foot-six-inch frame seemed to dwarf the six-foot man before her.

"What does it look like I'm doing, Becky? I'm having a late lunch," David Burns replied, taking a bite of a thick sandwich.

"Don't. Call. Me. *Becky*," she said through clenched teeth. "I hate that name and you know it!"

Yes, he knew it, and David hid a snicker behind another bite. He also knew that would rile her, just like he planned, wanting to keep her off-balanced to cover his true motives. He really had planned to be out of there before she got home.

Becca walked up to him, grabbed the sandwich out of his hand, and threw it in the sink.

"Get out of my house!" she snarled at her startled ex.

"Now, now, Beck ... Becca, this is still *our* house: community property and all that's in it. Speaking of which, I've been meaning to talk to you about that: we really should get the house on the market soon." He smiled gently at her. He knew his roguish good looks always got her. His deep blue eyes and dark blond hair were irresistible to all women, or at least that's what he thought. And she did find him irresistible when they met back in college in the Business Psychology class. It was part of Becca's required classes for her degree but David was only auditing it; he didn't want to pay the tuition cost or do the boring homework, he just wanted the information—his cheap attitude toward life should have been a warning to her. David's charm and good looks overwhelmed her sensibility and after a ten-week courtship, they were married.

Becca Burns stared at David, not believing she really heard what he had said, and she smiled.

"First of all, David, this house is not community property and never has been, *because* it's not my house, it's in a trust. I've told you that a dozen times but then you never did pay much attention to what I had to say. My Aunt Elaine made sure the house wasn't mine because she never liked you. She said you were a con-man and she was right. I should have listened to her." Becca leaned her back against the modern black side-by-side refrigerator, hiding her clenched fists behind her.

"That's cruel, Becca, and I'll have my attorney check into that trust thing you said she did. See, I do listen to you, but there is still a matter of everything in here," David said, suddenly unsure of where he stood in their divorce proceedings.

"David, when was the last time you talked to your attorney?" Becca quietly asked.

"I ..."

"Because, *David*, we've been officially divorced for almost a month now, and because you failed to appear in court to override the power of attorney you gave him, your lawyer cut a deal to keep you out of *jail*: you relinquished any and all joint assets in lieu of my not pressing charges against you for bigamy." David flinched as if she'd slapped him.

"That's impossible! He was to call me to discuss any settlement."

"Not my problem, David." Becca crossed her arms over her chest.

"Be reasonable, Becca. I'm broke," he pleaded. Now on his feet, he opened his arms for her.

"Well, you've got a really nice car for someone who's broke." She slipped out of his reach. "Get out of my home and don't come back, David."

Smirking with arrogance, he grabbed the blue and red striped cloth grocery bag sitting on the table and turned to leave.

"Wait a minute!" Becca snatched the bag out of his hand, surprised at how heavy it was and emptied the contents on the table: a two-pound canister of coffee, pasta sauce plus a package of linguini, a loaf of Italian bread, and four frozen steaks; two bottles of red wine rolled precariously close to the edge. "You're stealing my food? Wait ... you've been stealing my groceries all along, haven't you? I thought maybe the kids were eating more, but no, you're just a thief on top of everything else. This is a new low for you, David. Get out!"

David's face grew hotter as he turned away from his wife—ex-wife—and he wasn't about to let her see how upset and embarrassed he was. Skipping down the two steps from the door to the cement garage floor as carefree as he could pretend, he spotted the remote on the bench. With a self-satisfied smirk, he grabbed the control and tossed it onto the passenger seat of his car as he backed out.

Becca paced back and forth in the large kitchen, anger, hurt and confusion rolling off her in sheets of pure frustrated energy. How could he stoop so low? *He's a narcissist,* her aunt's voice echoed in her head. *No one will ever come before his own selfish needs—not you, not the children, no one. You know that. You've seen that, time after time,* the voice continued.

"But what do I do now? How do I get past all of this?" Becca asked aloud, the hitch in her voice leaning toward a whimper. Aunt Elaine was silent.

ooo

Rita Martin stepped away from the kitchen sink where she had been doing dishes. She had seen Becca come home from shopping and was going to stop over after she finished cleaning up the kitchen. That is until she saw the other car parked in the garage. Becca's house was well hidden except for the driveway that lined up perfectly with Rita's kitchen window. A few minutes later, she saw David leave and he didn't look at all happy. Rita dried her hands, grabbed her smokes out of habit, and sure that Becca would need some company, went in search of her best friend. Things in the Burns home had been tumultuous for over a year, and Rita thought the divorce would end that—apparently not.

OOO

Not wanting to surprise her friend, Rita knocked on the front door instead of just walking in like she normally did. After a moment, Becca angrily yanked the door open.

"What now? Oh, I'm sorry, Rita, come on in. I thought it was ..."

"I saw David leave. That was one unhappy man."

"Can you believe he didn't know our divorce was final? And I caught him taking a bag full of food!" Becca went still. "I almost forgot—I've got groceries in the car!" They made two trips each to bring in all that was in the back of the car, one trip with the cooler balanced between them.

"Thanks, Rita," Becca said with a sniffle. She pursed her lips and started to empty the cooler into the refrigerator, trying to focus on the task to keep from crying. Her emotions seemed to be all over the place lately. With David gone, she was now alone and lonely. Alone she had been accustomed to, but lonely was something new.

"For as long as I've lived across the street, that man has always been a jerk," Rita said. "And he's not worth getting upset over." She held Becca by the shoulders. "Where are the kids?"

"Camp Luna, a long, two-week vacation with the church that started almost a week ago." Becca sighed and then smiled. "Not much of a retreat though, they're only on the other side of town, a few blocks at the most?"

"You know those are long blocks and they're camping out, roasting hotdogs, making s'mores, and are being watched by other adults. Not that they really need much supervision at sixteen and seventeen—or maybe they do." She laughed. "Oh, and the swimming to cool off from this heat I'm sure is heaven! Pun intended." They both laughed. "Why so long?" Rita asked seriously.

"It was so I could pull a couple of extra shifts at Walstroms," Becca said, frowning. "With David not paying his child support, it's been getting harder to make ends meet and that he's been stealing food hasn't helped any." A fresh scowl found its way to her face as that memory returned.

"Instead of working extra shifts at a cashiers pay, why aren't you working that business degree you have as one of their managers?" Rita felt instant guilt not offering Becca a loan; however, she was sure her friend would be offended if she did.

"I should, I know. Maybe when the kids are back in school next month," Becca replied. "And they really are old enough to be left alone."

"Damn right they are! Forget about that for now. Consider this the beginning of a girl's night out or in this case a girl's night *in*! And happy hour starts right now." Rita let go of Becca and got two wine glasses down from the wooden rack suspended over the black and gray marble counter, and then opened a bottle of red wine from the two-sided, temperature-controlled wine cooler nestled under the counter and within easy reach. She knew Becca's kitchen as well as she knew her own, maybe even better.

"By the way, Rita, I like the new haircut. Short looks good on you," Becca said.

"And it's a lot easier to take care of now and cooler too." Rita's gray eyes sparkled as she ran her fingers through the pixie cut; her coal-black hair shimmered in the fading afternoon sunlight and fell right back into place.

"I remember when we first met." Becca smiled, accepting the glass of wine. "It was the ninth grade. You were a skinny geek with short hair then too and you lived on the other side of town."

"Yeah, but as we were saying, even the other side of town isn't that far away in Kapac!" Rita splashed some wine into the other glass and sat. "Have I ever told you how much I really missed you when you went away to college?" She stared into the glass as if it had answers to her unasked questions. "And why didn't you get a management job right out of college?" she asked, steering the conversation back to work.

"We got married within weeks of graduation and then David was always moving us. It seemed that every six weeks he would find that *perfect job* in another town and we would move again. We were never in one place long enough for me to find a good job, and then once Sandy came along ..."

Rita fingered the pack of cigarettes sitting on the table.

"Hey, I thought you quit smoking!"

"I did."

"Then why the smokes?" Becca raised her eyebrows.

"Just a security blanket," Rita explained, looking around the room and slipping the pack of cigarettes into her pocket. "I love how this kitchen has changed from those days of baking cookies with your aunt, and now that you've added your own touch, it's even better." Rita swiftly changed the subject again, and reminiscing about her aunt always lifted Becca's spirits.

"It sure has changed, that's for sure!" Becca agreed. "When Uncle Joey died, Aunt Elaine was a completely different person. She used his substantial insurance money to make some overdue and necessary repairs, like a new roof and a new furnace. Then she was on a roll."

"I, for one, am really happy that new furnace included central air. The kids can have the lake." Rita laughed, fanning herself.

"I still remember that summer I came home after Uncle Joey died." Becca looked away in thought, searching for those not so recent memories. "What a shock it was to see all the trees gone and a road put in. That developer wasted no time in subdividing the hundred and forty acres she was willing to let go of. I've got to hand it to her though; all that money was spent wisely: updating the plumbing and the bathrooms, all new appliances when this kitchen was gutted and completely redone. She told me once, she'd always wanted to modernize, but Uncle Joey was really stingy and didn't want to spend the money." She tipped her glass to Rita, still skinny, still a geek, and now years older. "To Aunt Elaine, thank you and rest in peace."

"She did wonders for this house, and she also did wonders for the town. This subdivision makes up almost thirty percent of the residential town now. Luna Lake may draw people in, but now the town people can live in nice, affordable, relatively *new* homes and rent out their smaller homes to the summer tourists, drawing in even more people, adding a big shot in the arm to the economy. I wonder if she realized what she was doing," Rita said thoughtfully.

"Probably. Aunt Elaine rarely did anything without thinking it through completely."

ооо

Luna Lake, the life and soul of the small resort town of Kapac, was a spring-fed oval two miles wide and three miles long. Kapac proper formed a horseshoe around the southern narrow end, filled with lakefront restaurants, gift shops, motels, and long-term seasonal rentals, all anxious for the

June to September tourist, and the shorter winter season for the snowmobile trade that kept the nearly fifteen hundred residents busy—and employed. A second business district two blocks in and behind the park that faced the original residential area was the local repository for a small grocery, butcher shop, a self-serve gas station with an attached convenience store, a yarn shop, pet supplies, hardware store, beauty & barbershop, and a small general merchandise outlet. At the far north end of that road was a funeral home with a seldom-used cemetery and at the south end was a small daycare next to one of the two churches in town.

The other end of the lake, with the same pristine white sandy beach as the town side, was home to a large campground and was always filled with tents and motorhomes while the Lake Luna Ecumenical Retreat next door sported small, well-maintained cabins. A chain-link fence separated the two for the safety and peaceful reflection of the retreat dwellers.

Other small residential clusters sprawled outward out of necessity to keep employees and shop owners close. Gradually, the families needed schools nearby and as the population grew, a medical clinic and office complex took care of most needs. A Walstroms, with a greedy eye toward the captive rural audience, eventually came to town, driving out one of the only two small grocery stores that had been a mainstay for decades. The superstore was conveniently situated between Kapac and the city of Dresden and pulled daily business from both towns.

Highway 21 entered Kapac ten miles from the new Walstroms on the north side, then ran through the center of town and exited at the aging movie multiplex on the south side. Although many roads spun off of Highway 21, around Luna Lake, or snaking through the subdivisions, they all came back to the highway: one road in, same road out. No one minded.

CHAPTER TWO

August 4
Friday

Becca had posted herself a reminder note to wheel the trash out to the curb early. It was Sandy's chore, but with him at camp, all the chores fell on her. She glumly thought she needed to get used to that for when he went off to college next year. She was amazed and somewhat distraught at how quickly her two children had grown. Becca contemplated how she herself didn't feel that much older yet at the same time reminding herself of something she heard years earlier: mothers grew older on their children's birthdays, not on their own. Becca sighed, wondering where the years had gone.

Next on her list was to call an old classmate, the local handyman.

ooo

"Josh? Hi, it's Becca Burns."

"Hi, Becca, what can I do for you?" Josh Clarkston grinned shyly though Becca obviously couldn't see him. His heart sped up and hammered in his chest just at the thought of hearing from her. He knew he shouldn't be so infatuated with a married woman, but she was so beautiful and nice too, always had been, ever since they met in the tenth grade almost twenty-five years ago. He sighed, knowing he had kept his crush a secret all those years. He could still remember the first time he kissed her, playing spin-the-bottle at someone's birthday party. That's all it took to set his heart on fire. He was devastated when she came home from college, married.

"I'm hoping one of your many handyman talents includes being able to reprogram my garage door openers and my security locks," she explained.

"Oh, that's easy to do. Are you having security problems?" Josh asked delicately.

"Yes and no. My ex-husband has been letting himself into my house and that has to stop. Can you help me?"

"Of course, Becca, I'll be right over." Josh hung up the phone. *Ex*-husband?

Josh wasn't the brightest bulb in the box, as his father reminded him all too often, but he had a patient knack for fixing things. Knowing his son would someday need a profession, Jack Clarkston schooled his son as much as he could to be a functioning member of the community as the jack-of-all-trades he himself was. Every town needed a cheap Mr. Fix-It, and being a lifelong resident, Josh fit right in. He also blended in—at five foot ten, light brown hair, pale brown eyes, and slightly overweight, no one looked twice at him.

OOO

"There, all done. Now you need a new password," Josh said, putting his tools back in the small bag he carried in his aging repair van. He grinned when she smiled and made a little turn-around gesture with her finger and turned his back while Becca entered the new code in the door alarm console. "When was the last time this battery was changed?" he asked, leaving the access door open to the door security system once she was done.

"I really don't know, Josh. Whenever I brought it up, David said he'd take care of it." Becca frowned, knowing she had relied way too much on David's word for getting simple yet necessary things done.

Josh popped out the 9-volt battery and put a new one in. "Although the system is wired directly into your house power, the battery keeps everything running in case of an outage and should be changed yearly. And Becca, please remember, I'm only a few minutes away if you need anything or have any trouble."

"Thank you, Josh, that's good to know. I appreciate it." She rose up on her toes and kissed his cheek. "I hope you don't mind me leaning on you like this. I may need other things done soon, at least until I get used to doing things myself."

OOO

"I thought you already went grocery shopping," Rita said, buckling her seat belt.

"I did, but now I have to replace what David swiped," Becca said. "Last night, I took a really good look through the pantry, the cupboards, and my freezer. What a louse. He thought by pulling things to the front or rearranging items I wouldn't notice there wasn't anything behind them! I can't believe how stupid I was."

Rita wisely kept quiet.

"So what are you doing for the rest of the day?" she asked instead.

"I've got an appointment with my attorney in Dresden in a few hours. I need to clear some things up about the house and about David," Becca answered. "Don't worry, we have plenty of time to pick up a few more items—like the frozen pizzas the kids like—and replace things David took and then stop at the butcher's. Having to restock makes me angry, and I'd rather get that done so I can relax after talking to the lawyers."

"I thought the divorce would have taken care of everything with David," Rita said thoughtfully.

"It should, but I want to make sure I can legally keep him out of here and that he knows it."

○○○

After Becca Burns called for an appointment, Alex Thornton pulled her file to review, even though he knew it by heart.

Rebecca Altess was orphaned at the age of fourteen and came to Kapac to live with her mother's older sister, Elaine. Elaine and Joe Cooper had been friends of his for many years and after Joe died, Alex counseled Elaine pro bono. He read over her contracts with the land developer and added his thoughts when she wanted to leave her house to Becca. Becca was a kind, generous and thoughtful girl, not one that got into the usual teenage mischief. Elaine and Joe never had children and looked at their niece as the daughter they wished they'd had. The arrangement filled a need for all of them.

Over the years, Elaine confessed to him how much she disliked the man Becca had chosen to marry. Once Becca and David had moved in to care for her as her health failed, Elaine was more convinced than ever that a divorce was inevitable, sooner or later. Elaine's motivation was to protect Becca and her two young children from ever being without a home and instantly agreed when Alex suggested putting the house and the remaining twenty acres in an unbreakable trust, of which he himself had total control over. Becca couldn't be talked into selling the house by her husband if she didn't own it.

Alex also knew that Elaine insisted on a clause that the house would become Becca's if David was out of the picture.

Alex was more than certain that Becca was not aware of this provision.

When Becca came to him about a divorce, Alex handed her over to his partner, James Montro, who specialized in that delicate area of the law.

"Jim," Alex poked his head into the other office, "Rebecca Burns is on her way over with some questions about her house and David. You got a few minutes to sit in on the discussion? You might be able to better answer some of the questions."

"Of course," Jim answered, retrieving Becca's divorce file.

OOO

"Have a seat, Becca. I hope you don't mind that I've asked Jim to listen in while you tell me what's on your mind. If it involves David and any part of your divorce, he would be more helpful than me," Alex said, leading Becca into his office.

"Oh, I don't mind at all," she said, settling into one of the big comfy mahogany leather chairs that sat in front of the large, matching, leather-clad desk. Becca rapidly tapped her fingers on the arm of the chair.

"So, how are the kids?" Alex asked to break the conversation ice, noticing her fidgeting.

"They're great, as usual. Right now, they are spending a long vacation at Camp Luna with the church," she answered with a wistful smile. "Another thing I have to thank Elaine for."

"She was very wise and very careful with her money. Instead of giving the church an outright large donation, she wanted to pay for something particular and set up an account to pay the property taxes on the retreat every year. The church was rightfully thankful and now you, Sandy, and Meg have lifetime memberships to the retreat." He smiled, and then got down to business. "So, tell us what's on your mind."

"I caught David in my house yesterday," Becca stated, pursing her lips to keep her anger from escaping as she told them all that happened. "And when I had Josh come over to reprogram my door locks and the garage opener, I couldn't find the other remote, the one I took out of David's car. I think he took it off the workbench on the way out."

"And David actually was taking a bag full of food? You're sure it was your stuff in that bag?" Jim asked.

"I'm sure," Becca answered. "First of all, the boxes and jars were dated with a colored marker, which is what Aunt Elaine taught me to do, changing the color every month so I remembered to rotate, and I always repackage meat a certain way before freezing. It was my food, no doubt. And to top it off, it was all in one of my homemade cloth grocery bags. How more obvious could he be? Besides, he didn't protest having to leave it behind once I saw it."

The two attorneys were busy taking notes when Becca continued.

"I think he's been sneaking in and taking things for months now, including the small flat-screen TV from my bedroom. I almost never used it and didn't miss it for weeks. How do we stop him, Mr. Montro? I've changed the locks, but is that enough? And what about the child support he's supposed to be paying? He's so far behind I'm pulling double shifts just to make ends meet."

"I'll get a judge to sign a restraining order this afternoon. And that same judge can order an auto withdrawal from any wages or commissions he earns. Understand though, Becca, that this might make David angry instead of stopping him," Jim warned.

"Yeah, I know, and that scares me. *He* scares me. Right now, I don't feel safe in my own home."

"And don't worry about the house. Even if he succeeded in coercing or threatening you into selling, you can't—it isn't yours to sell," Alex reassured her.

"Go home, lock your doors, and maybe get your girlfriend Rita to stay with you. David should be served the restraining order later today, or at the latest tomorrow," Jim counseled her. "Is he still working at the real estate office here in Dresden?"

"As far as I know, yes."

OOO

As Jim put together the restraining order, he thought about his recent visit from Rita Martin and the changes she made to her will.

"These are some extreme changes, Ms. Martin. Are you sure you want to make them?" he had asked her.

"Yes, I'm sure. You know I'm an only child and Becca is not only my best friend but more like a sister to me. Ever since my mom died, I have no one to leave my stuff to. Is that a problem?" Rita asked.

"Of course not. You can leave your estate, which is substantial, to anyone you want. As your attorney and your friend, I do have to ask how your health is, considering your urgency in re-doing your will."

"I'm fine, Jim, really. And there's no urgency, I just don't like putting things off once I make up my mind."

OOO

"Rita, what are you doing tonight?" Becca asked her friend. She had returned from the legal meeting, stopped at Walstroms, and then immediately called her.

"I'm open to suggestions, why?"

"Just come on over at 6:00. I picked up roast chicken with extra sides and a tub of chocolate frozen yogurt," she answered.

"Chocolate? You almost never eat chocolate. This must be serious," Rita said, laughing.

OOO

They sat on the upper deck, enjoying the warm evening breeze, bowls of the frozen dessert starting to melt in the heat.

"David isn't going to like getting that restraining order." Rita scowled, making circles with her spoon in the remaining brown liquid.

"I know, and that's why you're here. David wouldn't dare try anything stupid with a witness," Becca confessed. "While I'm at work tomorrow, the new locks will keep him out—however, I'm prepared to bribe you with a steak dinner to come back over."

"No bribing necessary, girlfriend, but I accept anyway." Rita laughed and tipped her head back to look at the clear sky. "I hadn't noticed those chemtrails earlier."

"You mean the contrails?" Becca looked up at the puffy white streaks in the deep blue sky.

"Contrails are the condensation from the exhaust emitted by jets flying overhead, and they dissipate quickly. Look how those emissions just hang there." She pointed slightly to the west. "And notice the pattern—jets don't fly in that kind of formation without a reason. And look! You can even see that small silver speck. That's the jet. Watch it."

They both stared in silence at the sky as the jet emission stopped and the jet circled back to start another burst.

"The theory," Rita went on, "is that the heavier, longer-lasting trail consists of chemical or even biological agents known as geoengineering and it's being used for weather modification mostly but in the past has been used to experiment with population control and even psychological manipulation. Who knows what other health problems could be happening because of that?" She pointed up at the sky, thinking about her own health issues and relieved she finally updated her will.

Becca snickered. "You really believe that?"

"Tell you what, I'll bet your best bottle of red wine that the weather changes drastically over the next few days," Rita said with confidence, giving Becca a geeky grin.

"I'll take you up on that bet! The weather man has been saying we should have clear skies and sun for next weekend's Kapac Days!" Becca picked up the empty bowls and put them in the dishwasher.

CHAPTER THREE

August 5
Saturday

"Good evening. It's 5:00 and I'm Cynthia Thompson here at WROL TV, Dresden, filling in for Jane Barker while she's on maternity leave.

"Here in Dresden, the town council voted to turn on every third fire hydrant as a means for children to cool off from the summer heat; adults are, of course, welcome to join in the fun." Cynthia smiled into the camera. "This will continue for the month of August on every day the temperatures reach 90 degrees or higher. As an added bonus, the fire department gets to test the hydrants and make sure they are functioning to capacity to keep us all safe.

"Earlier today, the Fire Department Rescue Squad Marine Unit was called out to retrieve a camper whose air mattress had floated out to the middle of Luna Lake. Jon Jacobson apparently had fallen asleep and had drifted too far out to be seen. Mrs. Jacobson called 911, thinking her husband may have fallen off and drown. Fortunately, his only injuries involved a nasty sunburn and a scolding from a very worried wife; so, a happy ending to a potentially tragic event.

"Now over to meteorologist Don Drake for the weather. Please tell me this beautiful weather is going to continue," she said, giving him a genuine smile.

"That it is, Cynthia. And welcome to WROL." He turned his body toward the blue screen that would project the weather map to the viewers. "As you can see, there are zero cloud formations out to the west to ruin the upcoming festivities in Kapac. We have a low-pressure system hovering over Alberta that might dip far south early next week and cool us off some, but we will have to wait and see how that system develops."

"That's good news to me, Don. It's been too many years since I've been here for Kapac Days and the fireworks over Luna Lake."

Becca muted the TV as the local news ended and the national news came on, leading with the daily baseball scores. She frowned, trying to pull up memories of the pretty red-haired Cynthia Thompson, and failing, shrugged it off. It eased her mind knowing the kids were still at the church retreat and that those in charge would have shielded the children from anything unpleasant happening at the lake. *An adult falling asleep on an air mattress is just plain reckless*, she thought, *and sets a bad example to the younger generation.*

Becca stepped out onto the elevated wooden deck that covered the entrance to the walk-out basement below and lit the grill in preparation for dinner with Rita. She normally didn't fix extravagant meals for only herself, mostly because Walstroms wasn't known for their high-paying jobs, but after the last few days, she felt she deserved the grilled steak and baked potato that was on the menu.

The pounding on the front door pulled her attention away from the tranquil scene of her extensive lush and wild back yard.

"What the hell is this?" David yelled at her, waving a fist full of crumpled papers in her face and trying to force her to step back so he could gain entrance into the house.

"I'm going to assume those are the restraining orders I filed and that you are now in violation of," Becca said calmly, not feeling calm at all. Her heart hammered so loudly in her chest she was sure David could hear. *It is time to stand up to him*, she told herself, and she held her ground, gripping the inside doorknob as a lifeline.

"Why, Becca?" He actually sounded hurt.

"Because I need you to stay out of my life now and out of my house! I have enough trouble keeping our two teenagers fed on a cashier's paycheck. I can't continue to be feeding you and *your wife* too! And just telling you to stay away isn't working, David."

David glared at her and changed the subject away from his other wife. "I have a right to see my kids!" His anger rolled off him in waves.

"Yes, you do," she agreed, "just not here. You are not to come any closer to my house than the street end of the driveway. When we have arranged visitation, they will meet you down there. They've been asking when you're going to take them overnight, instead of only a few hours. And by the way, you are three months late in your child support."

His breathing came in short angry drags of air into his lungs and snorts going out. He struggled to control his temper, knowing the addition of an assault charge would be disastrous. "And by the way, there is something wrong with your garage opener." He mimicked her to push a few of her buttons.

"Oh, there is nothing wrong with it. I had it reprogrammed when you stole the remote—again. And all the lock codes have been changed too." Becca let go of the door and crossed her arms over her chest. "David, you are not welcome here, now leave before I call Casey and tell him you're violating the restraining order." David knew Casey, the undersheriff of Kapac, had gone to high school with Becca and knew him to be very pro women's legal rights. He stepped off the wide porch and turned on his heel.

Becca closed the heavy door when she was sure he was down the long driveway. Her hands trembled as she relocked the door and she leaned her head against the frame, willing herself to not cry. Hot angry tears threatened behind her clenched eyes.

She looked at the thawed steaks on the counter, put them back in the refrigerator and opened a bottle of wine instead. Rita was late.

OOO

Dr. Micah Jones leaned back in his old leather office chair to watch the peaceful scene of the boaters on Luna Lake and heard the chair squeak. He admonished himself for putting on the extra ten pounds he now carried. Back in Chicago, where he was born and lived most of his life, there were restaurants and delicatessens of every nature on every corner and the variety—and the walking—helped him maintain his weight with his sedentary life. With parking being costly, not to mention impossible, he walked nearly everywhere. Being a general practice doctor wasn't always a busy practice. People seemed to want a specialist for every little ache and pain, so he sat a lot.

When he was offered the practice of a retiring internist in a small town in Ohio, he jumped at the chance to be out of the city and more in touch with his patients. The offer included repayment of a decade-old debt he owed, one he thought had been forgotten about; he should have known better. His year-long girlfriend accepted his decision without a complaint and moved out the next day. Surprised as he was, he quickly realized he wasn't going to miss her.

Micah wasn't a particularly handsome man—more on the plain side. Only 5'10", with soft blue eyes and dull brown hair that was already starting to thin, he had a nice smile though, an endearing bedside manner, and in his late 40s, he already had excellent credentials in the medical field. What he lacked was drive. He was a good doctor, some would say a great doctor, but he had no family, not even a girlfriend anymore, no hobbies or any interests outside of medicine, and to be honest with himself, he didn't even have any real friends. What he was, was bored with his life.

Kapac, with its slow pace and lack of expectations, fit his lifestyle, mentally, emotionally and physically—except for the extra ten pounds. He decided he needed to do something about that and soon.

OOO

Rita Martin pushed her short sleeve back in place once the nurse removed the blood pressure cuff and after drawing blood. It was hard to take the time off from working; it was even harder concentrating when she didn't feel good. It was common knowledge that Rita was a freelance computer systems analyst and website builder and worked from home. The latest high-tech computers and super speed internet she had access to allowed her the flexibility and means of staying available and in contact with her clients all from her spare room. What no one knew was that Rita was also a hacker, and not *just* a hacker: she was one of the best. Many companies dealing with sensitive information—including banks, credit card companies, and the government—hired her to break into their systems and find the weak areas. She would then back out without taking, changing, disturbing, or even reading any files; her core honesty kept her in high demand. After one company, not believing she actually got into their system, refused to pay her, she started leaving behind a calling card: a Thor-like hammer to prove she'd *broken* into their system. When she showed it to them, they had to believe her. From that point on, she revised her terms: if she could not get into a system, there would be no charge. However, if she got in and proved it, as was usually the case, her clients were expected to send their payment within twenty-four hours. Once payment was received, she would remove the hammer and seal the hole for them at no additional charge. As additional insurance, in that hammer was installed a time-delayed virus that could crash the best of systems. The delay was to ensure it could never be traced back to her, but she was always paid and always removed it before the timer started its internal countdown. She never had to send a second notice.

Dr. Micah Jones did a quick sugar test on Rita's blood and frowned.

"According to your chart, Rita, you're on an insulin pump, is that correct?"

"Yes, for a couple of years now, and I haven't had any issues with it until recently. I just don't feel normal. What's wrong?" she asked. She'd only seen this new doctor a few times since her regular doctor retired, and the last time was only two weeks ago. She didn't mind the extra visits; the doctor was kind of cute, but it really cut into her usually busy day.

"It would seem you're experiencing minor diabetic keto-acidosis. You aren't getting enough insulin in simple terms," Dr. Jones answered. "Let me see your pump and I'll download the self-check information." He was quiet for a few moments while his laptop medical computer accepted the information. "And now where is your cannula site?" Rita lifted her pale green shirt to expose her flat belly where the port delivering her needed medication was embedded into her skin.

"Well, everything looks normal except for your sugar level. Have you been under unusual or extra stress lately?" he asked, gazing at her pretty face just a bit too long. He nervously glanced away.

"Yeah, even though I work from home, some of the work lately has been rather ... intense." She silently chuckled, knowing the government contracts were always intense.

"I'll give you an injection to boost your insulin level. If this doesn't help or you don't feel any different tomorrow, come back in."

"But it's the weekend. Are you going to be here?" Rita asked, concerned.

"Although my office will be closed, I'll be on duty downstairs at the clinic. Being the new kid on the block, I'm getting the weekend clinic duty. Now don't you worry," he gently patted her knee, "you know the clinic is open twenty-four hours a day, seven days a week, just with a much smaller staff on the weekends. Personally, I think the weekends are busier, but who am I to argue? Now go home, take a walk, have dinner, relax, forget about work. You'll be fine." His eyes lingered on her face again and he thought she had the cutest freckles that sprinkled across her nose and he longed to count them. Slowly. His eyes darted away from her face again, and he blushed at where his thoughts were leading him.

ooo

Rita unlocked her front door to hear the phone ringing. Hardly anyone used her landline and most of her clients didn't even know her real name much less her phone number; payments from these clients went into an untraceable offshore account. Anonymity was her safety net. That's when she remembered she turned off her cell while at the doctor's office.

"Hello?" she said, picking it up on the fourth ring.

"Hi!" Becca tried to sound cheerful. "Are you still coming for dinner?"

"Oh, shit! I forgot. I'll be right over." She hung up before Becca withdrew the offer. Rita was hungry. She had been so busy with this new contract that she had skipped lunch in favor of a candy bar, which probably added to the shift in her sugar level.

OOO

"I'm really sorry, Becca. I haven't been feeling up to par, so I went in to see Doc Jones," Rita explained. "My sugar has been too high. Even with the pump, sometimes there are adjustments that must be made, though the pump really has made my life a lot easier."

"How are you doing now?" Becca asked with real concern.

Rita grinned. "Much better. He gave me a booster shot. What's for dinner? I'm hungry!"

"Did you skip lunch again?" Becca asked sternly. She had been through this with Rita for many years before she got the insulin pump.

"Yeah, and I'm going to make up for it tonight!" Rita helped herself to a glass of the already half-empty wine bottle. "Did you start without me?" she asked, laughing.

"Yeah ... David was here, and he was really upset about the restraining order." Becca refilled her glass.

"Yeah, well, he should be more upset that you had to get one! So ... what's on the menu for tonight?" Rita asked, trying to steer the conversation away from Becca's ex-husband.

"Ribeye steaks and a salad with a new dressing: one cup of low-fat yogurt, one half cucumber peeled and chunked, and a healthy dose of wasabi, all tossed into the blender. It's really good as a dressing or a dip and it's low calorie, low fat, low carbs yet high in flavor," Becca answered, grinning.

Rita sighed. "I'm really lucky to have a friend that makes things I can safely eat."

"Oh, and grilled pears for dessert—no more ice cream for you."

Totally out of character, Rita got misty-eyed and turned away to hide her wavering emotions. She didn't have many friends because of her secretive nature, but Becca was always there for her and always had been. And even as close as Becca was, Rita couldn't confide in her the strange things going on.

When she left the doctor's earlier, she'd found a hammer in the front seat of her car and it wasn't hers. Nothing had been taken, disturbed, or damaged; just that hammer, and that was enough to freak her out.

"It's still warm out, are we inside or out?" she said with a slight hitch in her voice. The hammer was too much of a coincidence and it alarmed her.

Becca tilted her head slightly, realizing something was off with Rita. "I think grilling out and eating in with the a/c. How's that sound?"

"Perfect!" Rita replied enthusiastically, her sour mood fading as the sun lowered in the western sky, leaving streaks of flaming red, orange, and yellows in its wake.

"Thanks for coming over. This past week without the kids has been a bit lonely when I'm home and not working. I keep wondering how they're doing."

CHAPTER FOUR

Sanders and Omega Burns were born exactly one year apart and consequently shared a birthday. Meg hated her odd name, even though her mother had explained that it was Greek and exotic and meant the end or the last, and Meg was the last child she would have. Early in her marriage, Becca had decided that two children would be enough and had her tubes tied right after Meg's delivery, which disturbed David— he didn't like her making those kinds of major decisions without conferring with him first. Sandy, on the other hand, thought Sanders was awesome and would be a great name when he got older and out in the business world. For now, Sandy was a cool name and since that was the color of his hair, it was doubly cool. He looked a lot like his father, and he understood his father was a handsome man.

Sandy and Meg stared at each other across the dancing orange flames of the nightly bonfire that was a ritual regardless of the weather. Meg scowled at her brother. Earlier, Sandy had caught Meg trying to sneak over to the public campground, a place that was off-limits during their stay at the church retreat, and he had stopped her before the counselors found out. The Guardians, as the adults were referred to, were very strict about the teens mingling with the campers that had very little supervision and tended to be older than the teens under their care.

Sandy, 17 and tall for his age at six-foot, took being a big brother seriously—most of the time. He smiled at his 16-year-old little sister and wiggled his ears. She started to giggle, exactly what he was aiming for to break the tension between them.

"Are you flirting with that girl, Sandy?" Justin Taylor, his current bunkhouse buddy, asked. Justin was almost the opposite from Sandy in looks with dark short-cut hair and pale blue eyes. That's where the difference ended. Both young men were tall and athletic in build. They had both come to camp with their younger sisters, though Justin's sister was only five minutes younger than he was. For the most part, the boys and girls were kept busy with different camp activities.

"What? No!"

"She is really pretty. I sure wouldn't blame you!" Justin continued looking at Meg through the flickering flames, a small grin spreading from his lips.

Sandy looked at him with a stern face. "That's my little *sister!*" he growled.

"Oh, then can I flirt with her?"

"No! She is off-limits!" Sandy quickly added, "To you and everyone else!" Sandy knew his sister was pretty and while he had the fair hair and deep blue eyes of their father, Meg had those dark eyes that guys went for and long dark hair that fell in shiny waves, much like their mother. And it was *his* job, *his* responsibility to keep her safe from all those love-em-and-leave-em schmucks at the campground or the one sitting next to him.

Sandy stood, never taking his eyes off his sister, and walked around the end of the large fire pit. He put his arm around her shoulders as he sat and gave her an affectionate, gentle squeeze.

"I know, I know, Sandy, I wasn't supposed to go over there," Meg said with a sigh and rested her head on his shoulder.

"Even though it gets so darn boring here sometimes, thanks for watching out for me."

"That's the kind of things big brothers do."

"But Sandy," she argued, "you're taking the big brother thing a bit too far. I'm 16 years old and I've never even been on a date! Most of the girls at school think I'm weird, and most of the guys won't even talk to me because they're afraid you'll beat them up or something!"

"Really? That's great!"

"Maybe to you but not to me!" Meg lamented. "I'd really like to go to the homecoming dance this fall. With a guy. You know, like a real date?"

"Anyone in mind?" Sandy asked, forcing casualness into his voice.

"Not yet ... you mean you'll let me go?"

"If I approve of him, sure, we can double date."

Meg let out a groan.

"So what are you involved with tomorrow?" Sandy changed the subject; he didn't like the idea of Meg dating, but was inwardly thrilled that she thought *he* had to give her permission.

"I think it's basket weaving day," Meg answered glumly, tossing a small stick into the fire.

CHAPTER FIVE

August 6
Sunday 1:00 am

"Hey, I'm really sorry, sweetie," David Burns said. "My phone alarm just reminded me I have a closing in the morning that I forgot about and I haven't done any of the paperwork."

"But you promised we would have the entire night together," Lisa complained, sitting up in bed and pulling the floral sheet over her naked breasts.

"This is a really big deal to close and all the files are at the office. The listing commission alone will pay my bills for months and the sales commission will double it," he explained, not liking the whine in her voice. He finished putting his freshly polished shoes on, grabbed his leather briefcase, and closed the door behind him. Jumping from the frying pan into the fire suddenly had new meaning to him. Maybe it was time to dump this clingy girlfriend, although having a girlfriend with her own business was nice. It meant he didn't have to help support her, and he was stretched thin enough as it was.

David hadn't been unhappy in his marriage to Becca. He hadn't been happy either. She was a good wife and a great mother, and without having a house payment thanks to her aunt, David always had enough cash to do whatever he wanted, but he was bored with her. He lasted five years of marriage before the affairs started. He knew he was addicted to the thrill of the chase and the clandestine meetings, but that wore off after a few months. He'd end it and once again be the faithful husband. Becca never knew—not until Amy. That business trip to Vegas ten months ago ended with him drunk and married. Two wives—not good—and then it was two wives and a girlfriend. His second wife, Amy, a fiery redhead, lived in Dresden. Unfortunately, his girlfriend Lisa lived in Kapac.

2:30 am

A new moon and the lack of street lights made the night exceptionally dark along the open field studded stretch of the highway. The professional stunt driver came to a hard curve in Highway 21 and increased his speed. As he took the sharp curve, he twisted the steering wheel and the delivery van skidded, precariously tipping on two wheels, and then flipped on its side. The metal screeched in the otherwise quiet night and the vehicle came to a stop two feet from the shoulder. A family of nocturnal raccoons by the side of the road fled the obnoxious noise and hid in the heavy underbrush, the only witnesses to the accident.

At the same time, the windshield cracked, the unsecured back doors sprang open, spilling boxes and canisters out on to the pavement. The driver, his job done, unbuckled his protective harness that prevented any injuries and climbed out the open window. He reached back inside and removed all evidence of the harness and made his way to the car waiting for him a hundred yards down the road.

The driver of the car pulled out his disposable phone and dialed.

"911, what's your emergency?"

"Yeah, I was just heading south on Highway 21 and I saw a white van on its side a few miles past the Walstroms store," he said in a deep, faked southern accent. "I don't see no one but someone might wanna check it out." He then turned the phone off and tossed it out the window a mile further down the road.

"What is your location, sir?" the dispatcher asked to a dead phone.

The state police and an ambulance arrived on the scene within fifteen minutes, followed quickly by Casey White-Cloud, the undersheriff of Kapac.

With blue and red flashers lighting up the dark road, the men found the van empty and started searching the area for the possibly injured driver.

Casey, his long, shiny black hair discretely tied in a ponytail and tucked under his wide-brimmed hat, walked cautiously around the crumpled van. He swept his bright halogen flashlight into the remotest of corners. He was 50% Native American and his tracking and observation skills were honed instinct and were well respected. He moved slowly toward the opened back doors, taking in the spilled contents.

One of the state troopers came up behind him and stepped around to him to get a better view. Casey's left hand shot out quickly, plastering against the trooper's chest, stopping him cold.

"I wouldn't do that if I were you," Casey said calmly, flashing his light into the dark recesses of the vehicle's cargo area. "Find the captain and have him call for a HazMat team."

"What do you have, Casey?" Captain Bud O'Connor asked, alerted to the growing situation.

"These canisters have chemical and biological hazmat symbols on them. We need to back everyone up and shut the road down until a team can clean this up," Casey replied, pulling his hat off to wipe the sweat from his forehead and letting his hair free to hang down his back. The relative humidity was rising quickly, making the air stifling, even with the cooler breezes of the night.

O'Connor eyed the undersheriff. "Your town, your call, but you do know that the state will take charge over you if you sign off and as soon as clean up starts, the feds will move in."

"I know, Bud, but this is out of my league. That's why I'm passing it off to you now, and I'm okay with that as long as this is dealt with quickly and properly—just keep me in the loop." Casey gave his friend a tired smile. "I've been up for pushing 36 hours. I'm going home and get some sleep. Call me when you hear—or find—something." With his deputies off on bereavement leave, home right now was the back room of his office. "You know, Bud, if a spill had to happen somewhere, this would be the best place possible. Anyone coming from Dresden can easily be detoured on to CR510 and still get into Kapac on the other end of town or keep going. I'll set up a 'road closed ahead' and a detour sign at the other end of 510 before calling it a night."

"I'll take care of the closed road signage on this end. Go get some sleep, Casey," Bud said, nodding to his friend.

CHAPTER SIX

Sunday morning
9am

"We have breaking news. Good morning everyone, this is Cynthia Thompson at WROL TV in Dresden." She smoothly turned toward the second camera and smiled. "At some point during the night, or rather early this morning, somewhere between 2:00 and 2:30 am, a vehicle traveling on westbound Highway 21 lost control and flipped over spilling its contents. The scene of the accident is located five miles south of the Walstroms and five miles north of Kapac, and it has been cordoned off while law enforcement continues their search for the driver. From the limited information we have received, the delivery van was carrying hazardous material and some of the canisters may have ruptured. A federal HazMat team has been called in."

"What does this mean for the town of Kapac, Cynthia?" Don Drake asked.

"For that, let's go to our in the field reporter, John Tasen," she answered.

"Good morning, Cynthia. I'm here at the sheriff's office with undersheriff Casey WhiteCloud. What can you tell us, Sheriff?"

"I can't tell you much since this is an ongoing investigation. However, a 911 call was received at approximately 2:30

am from a driver traveling south on westbound Highway 21 who spotted the overturned vehicle and called it in. As Cynthia pointed out, this is a HazMat situation and Highway 21 is now closed off to through traffic with a detour onto County Road 510," Casey said.

"What about the driver?"

"The driver of the delivery van has not been located yet. Now that it's daylight, we hope the search will be easier and we can get this person some medical help if needed. Thank you." Casey turned quickly and went back into his office. He didn't let that reporter see the scowl; something smelled off about this whole thing. How the cargo got loose meant the storage and transportation was just plain sloppy and that was highly unlikely for hazardous material.

"This is John Tasen on location from Kapac. Back to you, Cynthia," John said.

"Thank you, John. Keep us informed."

OOO

Being the seasoned field reporter that he was, John knew a big story when he saw it, and this could be a career-maker.

"Come on, Harry," he said to his cameraman, "we're going to be here for a few days, so let's find a motel on the main drag to set up in. We really need to stay on top of this story!"

OOO

Becca stood still watching as the TV went to a commercial. "I wonder what they mean by closed off to through traffic?" she said aloud. "I'm supposed to be at work in an hour!"

About thirty-five minutes later, Becca approached the area and saw the road blocked with military vehicles. She slowed and approached cautiously.

When a soldier carrying an M-4 carbine walked up to her car, she said, "Is there any way around? I have to get to my job at Walstroms."

"Sorry, ma'am, we are under orders that no one is to leave or enter the area. Please turn around and return home," he said and stepped back.

"Wait! What do you mean we can't leave the area? What's going on?"

"There is a hazardous biological spill, ma'am, and until it's determined whether the biological agent is contagious and who is responsible, Kapac is in lockdown. Now, please, go home."

Becca was stunned. She made a tight U-turn and headed for the other end of town. Becca had lived in Kapac for most of her life and she knew the roads well, especially the remote roads, and that's what she was looking for now.

County Road 510 was a rutted dirt and gravel road that looped around the outside of Kapac to the north where it gave access to the few farms that serviced the area with fresh seasonal produce and eggs. It was also a favorite road of the teenaged crowd for its remoteness and lack of street lights. Several turnouts were very busy during the late nights of summer for the spectacular starry sky ... and other things. Becca grinned at a few memories that surfaced as she made her way along Highway 21 to the secluded turn off, only to be stopped by another military-manned roadblock. County Road 510 was currently inaccessible.

She pulled to the side and pondered what the roadblocks may mean to the town and how long they would last. Becca headed back to town to Lake Luna Road and the sheriff's office.

"Casey? Are you here?" she called out.

"Back here manning the phones!" he answered.

"What are you doing answering the phones? Where's Judi?" Becca smiled fondly at her longtime friend.

"Hi, Becca." Casey's demeanor softened at the sight of her. There was a time in high school when they were more than just friends. When she came back from college married, he accepted that they would never pick up where they left off, though she still had a place in his heart. "Judi was visiting her mother in Dresden for the weekend, and now she can't get past the roadblocks, and I'm stuck without my secretary."

"Yeah, I left for Walstroms and was turned back on both ends of town by the military. What's going on, Casey?"

"Military? They sure moved in fast. Bud was supposed to keep me in the loop on this spill." Casey didn't take well to being a forgotten officer of the law.

"The soldier that stopped me on the north end of town called it a 'biological agent' that might be contagious. Do you know what happened?" she prodded.

"I'm surprised he offered that kind of information. Have a seat, Becca." He pushed one of the metal chairs next to his desk toward her. "I was at the scene early this morning and dead on my feet after being up over thirty hours running roughshod on some troublemakers at the campground. I left after the preliminary investigation to get some sleep. I handed off to Bud at the state police post, and he warned me that once the state police had it, the feds would likely move in."

"They superseded your jurisdiction? That's not right," Becca said.

"It's okay as long as that spill is handled and quickly. I'm not equipped to deal with what I saw." Casey briefly closed his dark eyes and rubbed the bridge of his nose.

"What did you see?" she asked carefully.

"This is nothing that isn't already on the news, Becca, but I saw several canisters with hazardous contents symbols, both biological and chemical contaminants. And although I didn't get real close, every canister I did see was ruptured or just plain open and *that* part is not general knowledge." He looked at her with pleading eyes. "Please stay away from there, okay?"

"Of course I will, Casey. I sure don't need anything else to worry about!"

"That reminds me ... I got a copy of the restraining order against David." Part of Casey's job in the small town was to stay aware of legal matters involving the population. He became aware of the Burns divorce weeks ago. "Is he bothering you?"

"Not in the last twelve hours," Becca snorted.

"Talk to me." Casey leaned his elbows on the desk toward her, his gaze devouring her beauty and his eyes brimming with warmth. Becca spilled a few tears of frustration along with spilling the recent events involving David.

"And then I had Josh over to change all the codes for the locks," she finished with a sigh.

"He comes by again, do not answer the door and call me immediately!" He slid his card to her with his private cellphone number written on the back, though he was fairly sure she already had it.

Casey gazed at her a moment too long and decided to press. "Can I ask you a personal question ... as a friend?"

"Sure," Becca answered with a slight lift of the edge of her mouth and a tilt of her head.

"Do you regret marrying David?"

Becca gave him a wide grin. "No, I don't. Without him, I wouldn't have Sandy and Meg, and I can't imagine my life without them—*exactly them*. I love my children deeply, Casey, and for that, I have no regrets at all." She paused. "What I *do* regret is that I didn't admit to myself sooner that our marriage wasn't what I had thought it was, or rather what it should have been, but I guess that's just part of the learning curve called life. I truly believe that everything that happens to us happens for a reason, how it should and when it should. And all I've been through with David has made me who I am right now. Personally, I like me." She gave him a wide grin.

"So do I," Casey replied, returning her smile.

OOO

Becca pulled up her driveway and parked in the attached garage, already tired from the day that had barely started. With the kids still safely at the church retreat, she undressed from her work clothes and went back to bed for a short nap.

Three hours later, a deep roll of thunder woke her. Confused and sleep-muddled from now too much sleep, she reached for her thin cotton robe and made for the kitchen, intent on making a fresh pot of coffee. Another roll of thunder took her attention to the solid glass doors leading to the upper back deck.

The sky had turned an ominous dark gray and the clouds were tinged with a sickly yellow that spoke of the kind of weather that meant trouble. Becca stepped out onto the deck to get a better view of the sky and was suddenly met with a deluge of heavy drops of hot rain.

Retreating inside, she poured herself a cup of fresh coffee. "I guess I owe you a bottle of wine, Rita," she thought aloud as a brilliant flash of lightning was quickly followed by a ground-shaking peal of thunder.

She stood for so long, mesmerized by the sheets of rain now violently pounding the roof and parched lawn, that when she finally took a sip of coffee, it had turned cold.

Becca dumped the cold coffee into the sink, rinsed her cup, and realizing how late it was, sought out fresh clothes to put on.

Back in the kitchen, she looked around. "As long as I've got an unscheduled day off—and unpaid—I may as well make the most of it." She set about to make a homemade pasta sauce that would simmer all day and Italian bread to go with it.

OOO

"Wow, it sure does smell good in here!" Rita said after shaking the raindrops off her umbrella on the covered front porch. Hours of pounding rain had left the air heavy with lung-crushing humidity and the ground slick with puddles of summer rain.

"Did you come by to collect your bottle of wine?" Becca snorted.

"Sometimes I hate being right," Rita said, laughing. "I was hoping this rain would cool us off some, but it feels as warm as ever."

Becca glanced at the outdoor thermometer. "It's 92 degrees outside and I would imagine the humidity is higher."

"Yeah, like 100 percent!" Rita snickered.

"I've never asked, but did you finally get an air conditioner?" Becca asked, rightfully concerned.

"I have a window unit for my office. A lot of my equipment is pretty sensitive, as are my files," Rita admitted. "And before you ask, I have a very comfortable couch in there to sleep on if it's really hot."

"Okay, but you know you are always welcome to stay here. There are those two unused bedrooms upstairs. I'm sure you remember this is a four-bedroom house, all of them upstairs. I'm using the downstairs den we converted into a bedroom that would accommodate Aunt Elaine's wheelchair when she couldn't make it up the stairs anymore. After she died, I took it as my room, in part to feel closer to her, in part because David and I ..."

"We're not talking about David tonight!" Rita said, cutting her off. "So is that delectable smelling sauce part of tonight's dinner?"

"Yes, and my best red wine just happens to be an Italian chianti. If you'll open it, it should breathe for a bit." Becca stirred the sauce then turned to her friend. "How are you feeling, Rita?"

"I feel great. That booster shot did the trick," Rita admitted, hiding her own trepidation about her health behind a radiant smile. "Would you like me to set the table?"

OOO

After dinner, they took the near-empty bottle of wine out to the covered front porch to relax and watched the rain as it continued to pound the pavement.

OOO

"Bud, this is Casey WhiteCloud. I thought you were going to keep me in the loop about this toxic spill," he snarled into the phone.

"I was just about to give you a call," Bud replied. "The feds should be on this by the end of the day."

"End of the day? The military is already here and locked down the town, Bud. They're calling it a quarantine." Casey lightened up. Apparently, Bud didn't know much either as evidenced by the silence.

"Military? Sorry, Casey, I really didn't know. How are things in town?"

"Quiet so far, but I'm here alone and things could get out of hand really fast if that was known," Casey said.

"What do you mean alone? You've got two deputies, don't you? Brothers, if I recall?" Bud replied.

"They're both at their father's funeral in Appleton; which, by the way, is where the entire town council is—at a training session of some sort." Casey hated what he had to do next. "Is there any way you can get me a couple of men? Just for a few days?"

"I'll try, Casey, but if the town is in quarantine, the state police might not be able to get through either."

"I understand, Bud. Do what you can. I also need a favor. Since I can't get out, and the mayor isn't answering his phone, I need you to be my eyes and ears on the outside."

"We've been friends a long time, Casey—I'll get you whatever information I can," Bud promised.

"Great. Ask around and find out why both sides of town are closed off. I understand at the spill site, but why keep the residents hostage like this?"

"That's easy: not only are they concerned that some communicable disease might be loose, they are now thinking it was an act of terrorism and that the perpetrators are still in Kapac. I don't think that warrants a quarantine, but now that the feds are here, it's out of my hands."

"Crap," Casey muttered.

CHAPTER SEVEN

August 7
Monday

John and Margi Maguire sat on the old yet recently painted porch swing on the wide, sheltered, wrap-around veranda that overlooked Luna Lake, enjoying an early morning cup of fresh-brewed coffee. Already unseasonably warm and on the way to brutally hot, they both had dressed in knee-length shorts and bright blue T-shirts that announced 'Kapac Days' in black script.

The Maguires had bought and run The Kapac House Bed and Breakfast over twenty years earlier and were now looking forward to retirement. The coming weekend would be their last Kapac Days, and they were already booked to capacity. John's breakfasts were well known among their regulars and they never had trouble filling a vacancy. On occasion when things were slow, they even opened for Sunday brunch for the locals. John loved to cook.

"I'm going to miss this," Margi lamented, still gazing out at the lake and the soft haze that hung near the shore.

"We don't have to retire yet ... not if you don't want to. After all, we don't even have a buyer for the place," John answered. "In fact, what do you think if we just cut back on when we're open to ease up on ourselves." Earlier in the summer, they had celebrated paying off the mortgage by deciding to retire from the hospitality business.

"Actually, that sounds like a good alternative, John. What if we're open only for holidays, like Valentine's Day, Easter...?"

"You remember the last time we did an Easter egg hunt—for the adults?" he asked, laughing. "We hid plastic eggs and two of them had gift certificates for a free weekend. They loved that."

"We could open for Memorial Day and the 4th of July for the parades!"

"And of course Kapac Days, Halloween, Thanksgiving, Christmas, and New Year's Eve." He silently counted in his head. "That's nine weekends out of fifty-two. I think I could handle that, what about you?" John was serious again.

"You know, that would make life running a B&B fun again," Margi said, smiling.

"I think you just like throwing parties as much as I like cooking for them," John chided her.

"I will admit that our Halloween party is a really big hit every year." Margi got lost in thought for a moment. "And if we really got bored, we could host one of those murder games. I think this could work for us, John. I'm not ready to move to Florida like a snowbird. Let's try cutting back and talk about retiring another time."

OOO

General Samuel Kapac served in the Civil War for the entire four years of its duration. Under the new president, Andrew Johnson, he was awarded a large track of land for his service and devotion to his country. Such gifting was a common practice from governments that could afford no other means of payments to the officers of their armies. He asked for and received nearly five thousand acres that surrounded a pristine lake in his home state of Ohio. The first time General Kapac saw the lake was during a full moon and that moonlight shimmered all night long on the still waters. In the morning, General Kapac named the beautiful water Luna Lake and he settled down, immediately starting to build a large house that he had hoped would become a home to his growing family.

Slowly, the general sold off pieces of land to support his family and the town of Kapac came into existence. The massive two-story house—with its eight bedrooms, servant quarters, two kitchens and three sitting rooms that were all graced with spectacular pillars and the wide wrap-around porch—was passed down to each generation until the last of General Kapac's descendants sold the house and moved away.

In the late 1960s, nearly one hundred years after being built, the Kapac House Bed & Breakfast came into existence. Remodeled several times, the eight bedrooms became six to include indoor plumbing, a more modern kitchen, and living quarters for the proprietors that encompassed one of the sitting rooms. Regardless, the historic building was still quite large and had a place of honor and prominence on the shore of Luna Lake.

CHAPTER EIGHT

August 8
Tuesday

Casey WhiteCloud sat at his desk in the cool office of the municipal building, a very empty municipal building. There were times when he relished the quiet and solitude, but today was not one of those days. There was too much to do, too much to contemplate, and he was the only one in the quiet building.

He picked up the paperwork strewn across his desk, hoping to make some sense of this lockdown, but it *still* didn't make sense. Even if they were concerned with terrorism, why lock down the entire town when only a small portion of the outskirts was affected? He set the papers aside and glanced at the double-windowed picture frame sitting on his desk within easy reach. On one side was a photo of his family: father, mother, himself, and his younger brother, taken a year before his mother died of cancer. On the other side was the photo taken prom night of him in a rented tuxedo with blue ruffles on the shirt and Becca in a robin's egg blue, floor-length gown, her rich brown hair piled on her head with tendrils falling to her shoulders. It reminded him of the happiest night of his life. She was so beautiful that night. Casey saw her when he was on patrol last week walking and laughing with Rita on the Boulevard. She was even more beautiful now.

He ran his finger gently down the photo of his family. His father, Jared, a name he picked for himself meaning one who rules; the full-blooded Native American was tall and proud, and looked every bit the chieftain he was. He had done well for himself and now had a lucrative dental practice. Casey's mother, Adelaide, with her ivory skin and strawberry-blonde hair, was a complete opposite, yet their marriage had been as solid as the ceremonial rock their wedding was performed on. They were a beautiful couple and produced two handsome sons. The cancer that took his mother was fast and aggressive, and Casey had barely made it home from the Army in time to say goodbye. Born Kesegowaase, or swift one, Casey also chose his own name when he became a man at the age of ten after he killed his first bear. Casey meant brave, and his father told him he was brave to face the bear alone. His brother, Wade, born Wanageeska, or white spirit, was in his first year of college when their mother died and it almost destroyed him if not for their father. Jared was Wade's rock; the Army was Casey's. Wade finished school and joined their father's practice as an orthodontist. Casey was proud of his family. When his father and brother moved to another, bigger town, Casey stayed in Kapac—it was his home. His father and brother honored their heritage by volunteering their services two days every month to those who remained on the reservation. Love of country and community was strong in the family.

ooo

"Hi, Casey," Becca said, stepping into the cool air-conditioned sheriff's office. "I still can't get through the roadblocks and I'm used to being busy. Could you use some help with the phones?"

"Seriously? You're a life saver, Becca! I really need to spend an hour or two on rounds," Casey said, relieved at her offer, as he casually slipped the picture frame into a drawer.

"Let me show you a few things." He explained the office to patrol car radio system, the preferred method of answering calls, and most important of all, where the coffee was.

"How long will you be gone?" she asked tentatively.

"I promise I will swing back around at least once an hour. If anything really major happens, call me on the radio and I'll head right back." He stopped half way out the door. "Thanks, Becca. I really, really appreciate this."

"I'm glad to help, but why aren't the mayor and the township staff here during this crisis?" Becca asked.

"The entire township board left on Friday for a conference in Appleton. Now they can't get back in. I sure hope this ends soon; I'm the only one here!"

OOO

Jessica Nelson cautiously pushed open the heavy glass door to the small butcher shop, happy to see it still open and the owner behind the counter slicing meat.

"Hi, John. Am I ever glad to see you still open," the church camp manager said with obvious relief.

"Well, now, Jess, why wouldn't I be open? It's the beginning of a busy week," John Mins replied. "What can I get for you?"

"I need lunch meat and lots of it and bread to make sandwiches for the kids, maybe some hotdogs and hamburger too. I've got two dozen teenagers that are starting to get hungry," she said, handing him a slip of paper that itemized her order.

John looked confused as he started slicing the meat on her list: several pounds each of salami, ham, turkey, and baloney, plus cheeses. "I thought the church had a contract with Walstroms for all the food for the retreat, including free daily delivery."

"Well, yeah, but ... haven't you heard what's going on?" Jessica asked. "It's all over the news." She scanned the shop to see what else she could use and picked out a few bottles of mustard, catsup, and mayonnaise.

"I never watch the news. Half the time you can't believe what they say and the other half you know they're lying." He bellowed a hearty laugh. "What is it this time?" He finished slicing all the meat and started on the order of cheese, while Jessica piled a dozen loaves of bread, buns, and chips into a box. *This was going to be his biggest order this week*, he thought, grinning.

She stared at him disbelieving. "Kapac is in lockdown. There was a toxic spill near Walstroms. No one is allowed in or out of town, and that means no deliveries either, so we're not getting any food to feed all those kids and no deliveries to Linden's Grocery to feed the rest of us."

John raised his head, yet kept his alarm to himself, forcing a neutral face. "No wonder my order didn't show up this morning. I thought they were only running late."

Jessica handed over the church debit card to pay for what may be only two or three days of food.

John helped her load everything into the church van; it was the least he could do for such a big order—and for the information. As Jessica drove away, John stepped back into his small shop, locked the door, pulled the shades down against the increasing heat and prying eyes, and turned the open sign to read closed. Out the back door, he began loading his personal minivan with food to take home. Then he put the rest of the fresh meats and the tubes of luncheon meats into the walk-in freezer, the cheese and remaining baked goods into the walk-in cooler, and he padlocked both. After grabbing the rest of the bread he left out for himself and a few bags of chips, he was done.

John had moved to Kapac back in the early '70s. After living through the 1967 riots in Detroit, he wanted out of the big city. His shop was on Gratiot and French roads, and he was always busy; it was a good life for several years. That intersection though was way too close to the fighting. Not one to scare easy, the riots were unlike anything he had ever seen: people shooting their friends, burning down their own neighborhoods, but the anger was the worst. He lived a peaceful life now but the memory of how violent some people got when they were angry and hungry never left him. He locked the back door and went home to ride out the lockdown.

OOO

David Burns had lied to Lisa about the Sunday closing; they never closed anything on a Sunday—banks weren't open and neither was the title company. He had just wanted to be away from her. He finally finished the closing at the real estate office as was scheduled for that Monday and at the bank, he deposited his healthy commission check in a private account, one neither of his wives knew about. He silently shook his head and reminded himself that Becca was no longer his wife—that would take some getting used to. They had been married for eighteen years. And since Amy was angry with him—again—damn redheads—he decided to head back to Kapac and patch things up with Lisa. Unknown to David, it was the last full check he would receive for quite a while: the order to withhold his commissions until the back child support was paid was still sitting in a sealed envelope on the accountant's desk.

A few minutes after passing Walstroms, David saw the flashing lights of a roadblock.

"What's going on?" he asked the soldier who had walked up to his window.

"You need to either turn around, sir, and go back or take the detour around Kapac. This road is closed." The young man pointed to the dirt road off to the right where several vehicles had already begun to take.

"Sure, but what happened?" David pushed.

"There was a toxic spill yesterday and the town is in quarantine. Now please, sir, go home or take the detour."

David was familiar with 510 and knew a short cut once he got out of sight. What he didn't bargain for was military personnel posted every quarter mile along the detour. He couldn't leave 510 without being spotted. Once he made it back to Highway 21, he pulled over to call Lisa. The call went straight to voicemail and disconnected before he could leave a message.

Frustrated and confused, he turned around and went back to Dresden and the temperamental redhead that was now his wife.

OOO

Dr. Jones checked Rita's blood count again.

"I'm not sure what's going on with your sugar spiking like this, Rita," he said. "I think I'd like to disconnect your pump and put you back on injections while I send this pump in for a manufacturer's diagnosis."

"Injections? Man, I thought I was done with that," Rita complained, scowling.

"You still remember how though?"

"Of course I do. I did it for too many years." She frowned to his back as he rummaged through a cabinet.

"Here's a new kit. Stop at the pharmacy downstairs for more test strips and a supply of syringes. I'll also call them with a prescription for you, though this kit should last you a week. We will get to the bottom of this." He patted her knee like she was twelve and left the exam room.

Rita watched him leave the room. She found him very good looking and more attractive each time she came in. She wondered about his marital status, though she had quickly noticed he did not wear a wedding ring, but that didn't mean anything these days. She might be getting older, but she was single and could still appreciate a good-looking man.

"Umm, Dr. Jones, this may be inappropriate, but would you consider having lunch with me some time, or maybe dinner?" she asked tentatively when he stepped back into the room with the written prescription.

"Ah ... Ah," Micah stuttered.

"That's okay, it was a long shot," Rita said, shrugging.

"No, no, Rita, I'm flattered, it's ... as your doctor, it would be unethical for us to see each other on a social basis." He held her gaze for a moment before looking away without another word, embarrassed, heat burning his cheeks.

"I understand, really, just remember, if you ever change your mind, you are entitled to a life, too." Rita slipped out the door, totally embarrassed and wondering what had gotten into her.

CHAPTER NINE

Reporter John Tasen and his cameraman were looking for locals to interview and emerged from their motel room just in time to see the HazMat team pass by. Dressed in hooded white Kevlar biohazard suits and the one-piece eye/face masks, they were hard to miss.

"Wait!" John called out. "Excuse me, John Tasen with WROL. Can you tell me what's going on?" He shoved the microphone toward the man he had stopped, and Harry stepped back so the camera could get both of them in the shot.

"No filming," the man stated, looking from John to Harry. "Shut it down or we confiscate the camera."

John stilled for a moment and then turned to his cameraman, locking eyes with him. John reached out and pushed the camera gently so it pointed at the ground. "He said no filming."

They had worked together as a team for several years and Harry immediately understood what John was saying, using a silent code they had used before, and he left the camera running, aimed at the HazMat booted feet with the audio still on. It was as compliant as he would be.

"Okay, so what's the deal?" John said, the microphone casually lowered to his side, pointed forward, hoping to catch everything said.

"There was a toxic spill just outside of town."

"Yes, we're aware of that, but what happened and what was spilled?" John asked.

"We're not completely sure what was in the containers. However, every one of them was either damaged or intentionally opened, including one that was marked as a sample of the Zika virus, complete with a few dead mosquitoes inside. The rest appeared to have escaped," hazmat explained.

John paled. "What about the driver? Is the search still on?"

"We have not found any trace of the occupants, which has led us to believe this was an intentional terrorist attack."

"Terrorists? But who and why?" John stammered, his heart rate accelerating with the news.

"No one has claimed responsibility yet." HazMat man turned to leave then stopped. "We will fog the entire town for flying insects as soon as we get the necessary supplies and equipment. Once we start, everyone needs to stay inside for 24 hours—including you." He hurried to catch up to the rest of the team that was informing the business owners of the fogging.

OOO

In the newsroom, Cynthia Thompson watched the incoming feed as it switched to filming the ground. She silenced the audio to the newsroom and cut the visual, yet continued to listen through her personal earpiece.

"There seems to be a minor technical problem. We will return with the weather after this short commercial break," she said to the audience with a casual smile. Standing, she slowly moved to the back of the room and turned her mic back on.

"John, are you still with me?" she said quietly.

"Yeah, did you get all that?" John asked excitedly.

"I sure did. You did great. Now the two of you better get some supplies and stay in your rooms."

"Supplies?"

"Food, you nitwit! You're going to be in isolation for at least 24 hours." Cynthia disconnected the call. She sat down at her news desk, made a few notes about the conversation, and with a sly smirk, deleted all the recordings Tasen had covertly sent, then set a block on any further feed from him.

ooo

John and Harry dropped the camera and the rest of their recording equipment in their efficiency room at the Luna Beach Motel and walked across the street to the sub shop.

"What can I get for you today?" the perky young girl behind the counter asked, smiling brightly. Her name tag read Cathy.

"I think we'll get six of the foot-long subs to go. Make it a variety and on different breads. You can put lettuce on all of them but can we get the tomatoes, pickles, and onions in containers?" John said.

"And those yellow peppers. I like those," Harry chirped in, grinning.

"What about dressing?" she asked.

"You got any packets? Those will be fine," he replied to her nod. "And when you cut them in half, would you please wrap them separately?"

After dropping the sandwiches off in their motel room that included a small refrigerator, a single burner hot plate and a coffee pot, the two got into the TV van and drove around looking for a gas station/convenience store, where they filled up on gas. Inside, Harry looked around and grabbed a cart, and then filled it with a Styrofoam cooler, a bag of ice, a case of water, and a case of beer. He added a couple bags of chips and pretzels.

John looked at the cart. "What are you doing, Harry? We have a refrigerator."

"Trust me," Harry said.

John paid for everything with the company credit card.

OOO

Tyler "Ty" Wanes was a big kid with a mean streak. Being bullied as a skinny runt when he was twelve, he turned into a bully himself as he got older and grew in size. Although he was almost twenty, he had only recently graduated high school, having been held back after a year in juvie for a crime he didn't commit. In juvie, he hit a growth spurt and grew six inches in height: he grew up, bulked up, and muscled up. And he learned to fight.

One of the more compassionate guards at the Juvenile Detention Center for Boys noticed Tyler sitting alone during lunch and not eating, after being there only a week. The guard recognized the symptoms and took the boy to the clinic, and after a confirmation that Tyler had been raped repeatedly, the guard got him a new cellmate. Sam was a black, gentle giant and he protected the boy, forced him to eat to bulk up, showed him how to use the weight room, and taught him how to protect himself. Sam was released four months before Tyler, and in those remaining four months alone, Tyler turned mean to survive, and he found he enjoyed the power.

"So who has food to share this morning?" Ty asked, popping open a beer he had bought with a fake ID.

George Nye, Barry Anderson, and Wayne Adam all passed a scared look between them. They had been his *gang* for their last year of high school and did his homework for him so Ty could graduate. The teachers all knew and didn't care, as long as Ty was gone from the school. They also had all witnessed Ty's temper and no one wanted to be at the receiving end of it. Doug Gard was the last to show up and dropped a couple boxes of nutty donuts on the picnic table, plus a package of hotdogs and a loaf of bread.

"My man, Doug! Where did you get this?" Ty asked, grabbing a box of the donuts. He had a sweet tooth, and so far was unaware he was borderline diabetic from his bad eating habits.

"I was checking out the girls at the camp next door and saw the head wench unloading food from her van. Being the nice guy I am, I offered to give her a hand with those heavy boxes and managed to grab a few things for myself ... I mean for us."

"Maybe we should be taking a casual stroll around town and see what else might be ... available," Ty said, laughing. The others knew what he meant and joined in the laughter, working themselves up to some ... illegal entertainment and absconding. While not quite as mean as Ty, they were still well on the way to a criminal life.

OOO

Casey drove his scout car over to the Luna Landing Gas Station and filled the tank. Inside to sign for it on the township charge account, he noticed the growing number of empty shelves.

"Looks like things are already getting a bit lean, Colter," Casey said to the owner behind the counter.

"Yeah, without deliveries, I can't restock, and when people see the empty shelves, they panic-buy," he admitted.

"Have you had any problems?" Casey asked.

"Nothing I couldn't handle. Some boys were in from the campground for beer and junk food. When they didn't have enough cash, they walked out with the stuff and laughed at me."

"Well, don't put yourself in any danger. Close up if you feel the need," Casey advised.

"Yeah, I'll do that, but I'll stay open as long as possible, Sheriff. People need to see some normalcy right now."

ooo

"Sheriff's office," Becca answered on the second ring.

There was a slight pause at first. "Good morning, this is Captain Bud O'Connor with the state police. You don't sound like Judi, so who am I speaking with?"

"I'm Becca Burns, sir. I'm filling in for Judi. What can I help you with?" Becca replied.

"Is Sheriff WhiteCloud there?" Bud asked.

"No, sir, he's on rounds. Can I take a message?"

"Yes, would you tell him I'm sorry, but I can't get anyone through the barricades, and to please call me at his earliest convenience."

"Of course, sir. He should be returning within the hour. If this is an emergency, I could radio him," Becca offered.

"No, just have him call me, thanks." Bud disconnected without saying anything further.

When Casey tried to return Bud's call later, there was only a rapid busy signal.

CHAPTER TEN

August 9
Wednesday

"It's only been a few days since the town has gone into lock-down, and people are already fighting over food!" Casey said when Becca came in for her new morning shift. He set aside the reports that were filtering in.

"Way too many people have gotten accustomed to stopping somewhere on their way home from work to pick up something for dinner, and don't keep much at home anymore," Becca replied. "What's going on?"

"There's been an outbreak of thefts. Starting with the outer gas stations like Luna Landing. Mostly what was taken was beer and junk food, and when someone saw and wanted a share, the perps beat him up pretty badly. I already talked to Colter about closing up if he felt in danger."

Casey turned to her. "Are you doing okay for food?" he asked, concern etched deeply on his face.

She looked around even though she knew they were alone. "Yeah, I'm okay. Aunt Elaine was pretty adamant about keeping at least a month of food on hand at all times. It's gotten to be a habit for me now and I recently went shopping to fill in what David has been taking. So yes, I'm okay." Becca settled into her new place and rearranged the post-it note pads and pens. She smiled and waved at Casey as he left. And then the phones started ringing; it wasn't even 8:00 am.

As Casey left his office, the news crew from WROL was waiting for him. A microphone was shoved in his face.

"Sheriff WhiteCloud, do you have an update for us?" John Tasen asked.

"No, I don't." He turned away.

"Can you tell us when this lockdown will end?" Tasen persisted.

"No, I can't. When I know something, I'll be sure to find you. Excuse me." Casey pushed past the annoying newsmen and got in his squad car.

OOO

Sheriff WhiteCloud picked his usual route to start with: a quick cruise down the main drag of town, around through the subdivisions, letting him be seen by the locals, and occasionally waving hello to someone. After passing by the church, he decided to swing around Luna Lake and check out the retreat and the campground, which would take him by the multiplex and back to the main business district. It was another warm morning and the drive was soothing and his thoughts drifted to Becca and wondered if it was too soon after her divorce to ask her out.

Casey pulled to the south side of Highway 21 and stopped in the shade of a tree by Grayson Park to observe a group of vaguely familiar older teens. When one of the boys hefted a brick through the window of a closed store, he turned his flashers on, making a U-turn to confront the vandals.

"That's enough!" he said, stepping out of the patrol car, wishing he had back up. However, after Bud's message yesterday, he knew he had to handle this on his own.

"Well, if it isn't the long arm of the law. We're hungry, Sheriff. There's no food left at the campground store and most of these stores have closed, *and* there's no way for us to leave this damn town," one of the boys said. Now that he was closer, Casey recognized several of those that had already been causing trouble, especially their ringleader, Ty something.

"That does not give you the right to break into a privately owned business," Casey replied, keeping calm. "Now all of you line up, sit on the sidewalk, and let me see your hands." As he walked around the end of the car, one of the boys turned and fired a handgun in his direction.

ooo

It was 11:00 am when Casey stumbled through the front door of the building that housed the sheriff's and the township offices.

Becca bolted from her seat at the front desk to help him to the nearest chair.

"My God, Casey, what happened?" she asked, noticing the blood running down the left sleeve of his shirt.

"I probably should have gone straight to the clinic, but this was closer." He drew in a couple of deep breaths.

"Well, we're going to the clinic as soon as we do something about this bleeding!" Becca said. She quickly removed his tie, tossing it on the desk and unbuttoned his shirt, looking for the source of the blood that had spread up to his shoulder. Not finding the injury, she then pressed a thin, institutional beige towel against his arm, hoping to staunch the bloody flow. Faced with not knowing how to hold it place, she started going through the desk drawers for something to use. She wrapped the towel securely on with duct tape she found. "Casey, look at me!" she said, noticing his eyes fluttering. "What happened? The doctors will want to know."

"A couple of guys were smashing in the windows of Annie's Donuts. When I showed up, they turned and shot me. Same punks from the campground. I barely made it to the patrol car." He slumped further into the chair, closing his eyes against the pain, thinking movies made getting shot like it was nothing, when in reality it hurt like hell!

"Help me out here, Casey. I need to get you into my car, so stay awake!"

She looped Casey's arm around her neck and lifted him to standing. Together, they staggered out to her car.

"Lock the door, Becca. Too much in there," he murmured as the pain surged again and he collapsed in her front seat. She slammed the door closed, not caring if he dripped blood on her seats, then she went back inside and in less than a minute, made sure everything was turned off and the doors were locked, grabbing the keys from the scout car as an afterthought.

She sped past by Annie's Donut shop and saw several kids walking around, carrying boxes of baked goods and laughing.

The clinic was on the other side of the business district, normally a five-minute drive minimum, but Becca made it in two minutes, running a stoplight when she saw there was no cross traffic. After all, who was there to give her a ticket? Pulling under the emergency room portico, Becca blasted her horn before jumping out and rushing into the clinic.

"Hello? I need some help out here," she yelled. When no one answered, she grabbed one of the wheelchairs and rushed back to her car. It was a struggle for her to get Casey standing enough to get him into the chair, and she pushed him in through the sliding doors as a disheveled Dr. Micah Jones came from the back.

"Where is everyone?" Becca asked the doctor who by then had taken charge and wheeled Casey into one of the exam rooms.

"I'm afraid I'm it. None of the other doctors or nurses can get past the roadblocks," he replied. "Help me get him onto the table. Duct tape? Inventive but effective." The doctor snickered at the makeshift bandage, but said nothing else as he cut the towel loose and then cut the sleeve off. The sheriff was breathing through his teeth, grimacing from the pain. "What happened?"

"He was shot by some kids robbing a store," Becca answered.

"Sheriff, I'm going to give you a local anesthetic so I can remove the slug," Doc Jones explained as he worked. "There doesn't seem to be that many people in town," the doctor continued to talk casually to distract his patient. "I thought Kapac Days was a big deal around here."

"Oh, it is, but the festivities don't really start until Friday. Then everything happens all at once: there will be vendors lining both sides of the street, and everything stays open late. First thing on Friday morning, I block the road while vendors set up and detour the traffic around the park on to the Boulevard," Casey said, sucking air between his teeth and wincing at the sting of the hypodermic. "Those vendors, by the way, depend on Kapac Days for a large chunk of their income." The local soon took effect and Casey didn't feel the doctor digging around in his arm.

"What do they sell?"

"Local craft like baskets, blankets, beaded jewelry, and pottery. Farmers set up selling produce and eggs; some do baked goods. This year, we have a geode seller coming again, where you can select an egg-like rock and it gets split in front of you, exposing a variety of crystals inside. I hear there is even a fortune teller scheduled," Becca said excitedly, almost forgetting why they were in the clinic. "And in the past, Grayson Park is where the carnival sets up. There are a couple of rides, and mostly the cheesy games of chance. Everyone loves it though," Becca added, remembering the monkey Casey had won for her years ago. She still had it somewhere.

"Anything else? That doesn't seem like a lot." The doctor wanted to keep them talking and busy before the local he gave Casey wore off.

"Oh sure, there's art work, wood crafts, crocheted items, and a massage therapist is coming with a chair to do mini-massages. We had a stained glass guy last year, but he was ... strange. Arrogant and moody. So we didn't invite him back." Becca focused her attention back on how the sheriff was doing.

"Saturday afternoon is the parade down the center of Main Street, with the fire truck and ambulance; the kids do a lot of fun floats, and of course anything political that might be on the current ballot gets promoted," Casey continued. "And Saturday night are the fireworks over Luna Lake. By Sunday afternoon, everything is back to normal and most of the tourists have left."

"That's it?" Doc Jones questioned. "You seem to know a lot about it."

"Flyers on the vendors and the times for the activities are posted everywhere," Casey said. "Besides, I'm the sheriff. I know everything going on in town."

"It might not sound like much, but it's a big deal here," Becca added. "The sales alone are about a third of the yearly revenue for some. Plus, by Friday, all the motels are full, some are full already, and you'd be lucky to have only a half-hour wait at any of the restaurants."

With Becca's limited assistance, Dr. Jones had washed down the injury, extracted a .38 caliber slug from the sheriff's left bicep, and thoroughly irrigating it, he stitched the hole closed. After applying several gauze pads, he wound a self-adhesive bandage around the sheriff's upper arm and stepped back. Having a medical practice in Chicago gave him a variety of emergency room skills and too much practice removing bullets.

"How long will he have to stay here, Dr. Micah?" Becca asked, already on a first-name basis from having both kids in for their school physicals.

"He *can't* stay here, Becca. I'm the only one on duty. I can't take care of him and anyone else that comes in," he explained while attaching a sling around Casey's injury. "And Sheriff WhiteCloud will need around the clock observation for at least 48 hours."

"What am I supposed to do?" Becca whimpered, her previous optimism now overshadowed.

"Take him home with you if you have to." The doctor unlocked a cabinet and removed a couple of boxes. "Here, these are samples of a strong painkiller and antibiotics. Doses and directions are on the side of the box. Make sure he takes all these antibiotics, as bullets are notoriously filthy from being handled carelessly. Now go! HazMat was by earlier and said they will start spraying any time now. You have to get home and indoors."

ooo

"Oh, man, my whole arm really hurts!" Casey moaned when jarred from Becca stopping the car; the local had definitely worn off. She pulled as close to the house as possible.

"I'll give you a pain pill as soon as I get you in the house," Becca said. "These pills will knock you out and I need your help to get you moved. Now let's go."

She moved his legs around to the side and out the door, much like she did with Aunt Elaine. However, instead of grabbing both his arms to pull him upright, Becca pulled on his right arm enough to get him standing and then let him lean on her.

"Come on, Casey, one step. That's all it is to get on the porch." He took a deep breath and let her lead him in. Even all his years in the Army, he had never been shot; the pain was excruciating. Inside the house, his usually strong knees started to buckle. Becca let him slide down onto the nearest recliner.

"I think this is where you're going to stay, big guy!" Becca joked. She pushed the lever on the side to raise his feet. "I'll get you some water and you can take a pill." She turned away and muttered, "Sissy."

"I heard that," he growled. Becca turned back to see him grinning even though his eyes were still closed and she laughed.

After he took an antibiotic and the pain pill, Becca pushed on the chair until it was fully reclined and got two pillows: one for his head and one to support the sling holding his arm. Within minutes, Casey was asleep. She pulled his shoes off, dropping them on the floor, and then eased his service pistol out of its holster, setting it on the fireplace mantle behind a picture. Becca left him there while she pulled her car into the garage and sponged the long streak of still crimson blood off the seat.

OOO

John Tasen and his cameraman Harry cruised up and down the main street looking for anyone else to interview. The street was strangely empty so they turned up the next street and found themselves on the Boulevard.

"This has got to be one of the most boring towns we've been to," Harry commented.

"Hey, there's a grocery store that's still open. Let's go talk to them," John said.

OOO

John pushed the heavy glass door inward and felt a waft of cool air greet them. Harry followed, carrying the camera, thankful the equipment had made massive strides since they first became a team. The new cameras were lighter in weight, had all the different lenses built in, and this one came with its own telescoping Omnipod for keeping the camera steady while he filmed.

"Good afternoon," the older man behind the register said. "Can I help you find something?"

"I'm John Tasen with WROL."

"I know who you are. I recognize you from TV."

John couldn't help but grin from being recognized.

"We came to Kapac Sunday morning to cover the spill, and now we're stuck here just like everyone else," John explained. "I'm hoping to get some interviews to add local flavor to the story we will eventually air. Anything you can share with us?"

Harry brought the camera up and adjusted the focus.

"Not really. Most of the tourists don't know about us local merchants; they prefer to run to Walstroms for whatever they want. I pretty much service the people who live here. By the way, I'm Carl Linden. I own the place." After shaking hands, John looked around.

"You seem to still be well supplied," John said, gazing at the nearly full shelves.

"I recently restocked from the back," Carl said, laughing. "I keep a small on-hand inventory, unlike the bigger stores that are on the JIT system."

"What is the JIT system?"

"Just In Time. With inventories being kept on a computer and sales tied into that too, at the end of the day, a key is hit and the purchase order goes out to the various suppliers. Many times, delivery is made the next day: no reason to keep stock in the back room anymore and they do constant rotation," Carl explained. "Only what is sold is restocked. Makes it easier on cash flow."

"So you don't adhere to the ... JIT system?" John prodded.

"Nope, it's easy enough for me to know what sells and what doesn't, and what sells I keep extra of in the back. The shelves are always full in the morning." He gave them a knowing smile. "That being said, my back room is now empty, and what you see is it. The locals have been in and buying up essentials. It's hard to keep up with that kind of demand."

"What essentials?" John asked.

"Food, young man, food—shelf-stable food and toilet paper. If they overbuy right now, they will just buy less next week, but at least they will eat this week."

"Mind if we look around?" Harry asked.

"Go ahead, take a cart. You might find something you need." Carl smiled and went back to his seat behind the register.

Harry grabbed a cart, set his camera in the baby seat, and headed down an aisle.

"What are you doing, Harry?" John asked when he caught up to his cameraman.

"Something struck me with what the old man said, and it reminded me of a hunting trip with my dad several years ago." Harry stopped to pick a couple cans off a shelf. "Dad's hunting shack was a 12x12 foot room off a two-track road in the middle of nowhere, with bunk beds built onto one wall, a small table, two chairs, and a coal-burning potbellied stove. There were always a couple of cast iron pots hanging on the wall beneath a shelf that held tin plates. We were only going for a long weekend. Mom always packed our food for us and sometimes with stuff I didn't like, but she said was good for me. Anyway, our second day in there was a freak snow storm and we were socked in for days. If not for *shelf-stable* cans of food like the fruit cocktail she packed for us, we would've gotten real hungry real fast. I've actually grown rather fond of fruit cocktail now."

"You were there to hunt, why not just shoot something to eat?" John pointed out.

"With the storm, the deer had gone to ground. Nothing was moving." He stopped and took a couple more cans.

"What did you do?" John was now intrigued with Harry's story.

Harry laughed. "We played a lot of cribbage. And we rationed what food we had, eating the fresh stuff first."

"You mean like all the sub sandwiches?" John noted with a touch of irony in his voice.

"Yeah, only we didn't have refrigeration. And before you say something about it being cold outside, one does not leave food out that would attract bears or wolves. That's a recipe for disaster."

John looked at what Harry had put in the cart: cans of beef stew, ravioli, soup, and fruit cocktail—all things that could be eaten right from the can. "What are you going to do with all that if we get to go home tomorrow?"

Harry shrugged. "If we don't need it, we can give it to the local food bank. But what if we do need it? What if we metaphorically get snowed in for days and days? The sub sandwiches won't last very long. Will this be *enough*?" He nodded his head at the cart.

John thought for a few moments. "I suppose we should get some plastic forks and spoons ... and more water." Then he grabbed a couple cans of chicken and dumplings for the basket.

Harry rounded a corner near the front of the store.

"Mr. Linden, where would I find a can opener?"

"Aisle three," the old man pointed, "about halfway down on the right."

Coming up another row, Harry took a roll of paper towels and a box of drawstring plastic bags for the trash they were sure to create.

Mr. Linden watched the two men thoughtfully. "Are you two about done? I'm closing up soon. I need to be getting on home."

"I think this should do it, and thanks for taking the time to talk to us today."

After loading everything on the conveyor, John shook his head and whispered, "The accountant is going to kill me," and handed over the company debit card.

OOO

When the news crew left the store, Carl lowered the window shades, locked the front door, and turned out the lights. It didn't take much or long for him to decide to close up shop and wait this out. Like John Mins, Carl had lived through the riots of a big city, and he was suddenly very uneasy.

He walked past the coffin coolers, large display areas that kept meat and produce chilled, and seeing there was little left, went back to the front register. He took two of the bright blue souvenir cloth bags that said KAPAC DAYS in black script and filled one with the two remaining steaks, a package of cut-up chicken, a pot roast, and two dozen eggs, and then shut the cooler off to save on electricity. In the small produce section, he took the last head of lettuce and two trays of toma-toes—a salad would go nicely with one of those steaks. He shut that cooler off too.

Carl set the heavy bag near the swinging doors that led to the stock room and went back down the aisles, collecting various cans of beans, soup, and canned fruit.

Then he made his way to the very back where a set of stairs took him to his home, a spacious apartment above the store. The door leading up the stairs was paneled to match the surrounding walls and was near-invisible when closed. Carl closed and locked that door for the first time ever.

CHAPTER ELEVEN

August 10
Thursday morning

Lisa Eddington pushed her sweat-damp blonde hair off her forehead, tucking ends of it behind her ear. It was hot—really hot. The thermometer in her gift shop read 99 degrees, and that was in the shade at 8:00 am. The high humidity made the air outside almost unbreathable. The aging two-story house was left to her by her grandmother, who had started and run the gift shop in the front half of the first floor for many years. Living in the back half of the house like so many of the shop owners made it easy and inexpensive. The upper floor had been renovated as a rentable apartment that was currently vacant. Now it was all Lisa's.

Lisa saw Mrs. Ostrander from next door pulling her wagon down to the shore of Lake Luna, right on schedule. Every morning, the elderly lady filled a bucket of water and dragged the small, old wagon back to the house, twice. Lisa never asked the 75-year-old woman what she was doing; it was none of her business—until now.

Lisa watched as the old lady collapsed on the sandy beach. She bolted out the back door to help her struggling neighbor.

"Mrs. Ostrander, are you okay? Let me help you up." Lisa lifted the frail woman to her feet and bore her weight as they stumbled into the house.

"Oh, thank you, dear. I think the heat got to me," she said, leaning against the sink while the water ran cold and she splashed her face to cool off. A cloud of steel gray hair framed her wrinkled face, and short wisps of gray stuck to her forehead from the splash of water.

"You shouldn't be doing such a strenuous activity in this heat!" Lisa gently admonished her. "I'll bring your wagon up. You sit here."

Dragging the old wagon through the sand in the oppressive heat was difficult even for the young woman; how the old woman could do it surprised Lisa. "Where do you want this bucket?" she asked, setting the pail in the small kitchen.

"In the bathroom, if you don't mind."

When Lisa sat down opposite the old lady, she looked quizzical.

Mrs. Ostrander rolled her eyes. "I know you will think me crazy, most people do," she mumbled. "We are metered for our water, you know that. I'm on a very limited income and to save as much as I can, I use the lake water to flush the toilet, even sometimes to wash dishes."

Lisa smiled. "We all do what we have to do to get by. I know you always bring in two buckets. Would you like me to get the next one? You really shouldn't go back out in this heat."

The old woman looked at the youngster, who was less than half her age. "Thank you. I would appreciate that." Her voice quivered at the unexpected generosity.

Once Lisa set the second bucket down inside the house, she took the erasable marker off the board hanging on the ancient refrigerator and wrote her phone number in bold red marker.

"There's my phone number. If you need anything else done, call me! I'm right next door, Mrs. O."

"You're very kind, Lisa, and so very much like your grandmother. We were best friends for a long time."

"I know. Gram talked about you quite often. Now I really need to get back. I'm expecting a phone call." Lisa hadn't heard from David since he left early Sunday morning.

"Humph, from that David? He's not a good person, Lisa. He will bring you nothing but grief."

Thursday
Noon

Becca sat on a chair facing the sleeping sheriff.

"What am I supposed to do with you, Casey?" she asked. After toast and coffee, she had given him another dose of the medications and he had quickly faded out again, which allowed her to change the dressing without causing him further pain.

She watched his relaxed features and remembered another time when she watched him sleep. A melancholy smile reached her dark eyes as she remembered the boy behind the man. It was mid-June, their senior prom night, and Casey had driven them out on County Road 510 to one of the more remote spots. They gave each other their virginity that night and wrapped in each other's arms, they fell asleep in the back of Casey's truck after watching the stars come out. The following week, Casey left for boot camp and three years in the Army that turned into ten, and that fall, Becca went away to college.

Even before he was out of boot camp, Casey quickly gained attention when his potential was recognized and was selected for military police training. Furthering that when he was discharged, Casey joined the sheriff's department and over the years climbed the ranks and had settled into a career he loved. Becca had watched his career from afar with the fondness of an old, and close, friend.

OOO

Thursday
3:00 pm

Casey blinked his eyes open, feeling a bit groggy and disoriented. He stretched his arms and immediately regretted it. Pain shot through his left arm from his fingertips to his ear, or so it seemed, and everything came back to him.

"Becca?" he mumbled.

"Hey there, sleepyhead." She came in from the kitchen with a glass of iced tea. "How are you feeling?"

"Like someone hit me with a truck, backed up, and hit me again. I stink. I need a shower."

Becca helped him to stand and led him into her room. He looked around and raised his black eyebrows at her. "It's the only shower on this floor and I doubt you can handle the steps to get upstairs just yet," she answered with a smirk.

She unbuttoned his shirt as he watched her and when she stopped at his belt buckle, he cleared his throat and said, "I think I can get it from here," never taking his eyes off of her.

"I'll see what I can find for you to wear." Becca pulled her eyes from him, embarrassed, and went to search Sandy's room, while Casey turned on the water. He glanced around the spacious, pale green bathroom, noticing the feminine touches: floral shampoo, a small dish filled with scented soaps, colorful towels, and her hairbrush. With a sigh, he remembered how much he loved brushing her hair when they were young.

With a pair of thin cotton tan pants from Sandy's closet and a purple sleeveless muscle shirt from his drawer that advertised some obscure rock band, she set the clothes on her bed and called through the door, "I've set some clean clothes for you on the bed when you're done."

Ten minutes later, with only a towel around his waist, Casey stepped out of the bathroom feeling clean and refreshed. He put on the pants and after a struggle, called her in, "I can't lift my arm to get the shirt over my head. Any ideas?"

Becca stared at his bare, muscular chest which was still the color of dark honey like she remembered and now glistened damp from the shower. She swallowed, trying to keep her eyes on his face. He grinned. She lifted the large armhole over his injury first, and then pulled it over his wet head, then his other arm.

"Thank you, Becca."

"You're welcome."

"I want to see you again."

"Okay." She was lost in his dark smoky gray eyes and memories flooded her veins.

"Maybe take you to dinner?"

"Okay."

"Or a movie?"

"Okay."

"I want to kiss you."

"Okay."

He lowered his head and brushed his lips across hers, and she sighed, leaning into him, imagining herself melting, sliding to the floor in a puddle of hormones and liquid desire.

That did him in, and he kissed her with the passion from their shared youth. He exhaled a groan, resembling a rusty hinge.

"I want you."

"Okay."

He smiled and said, "When I'm better and can hold you with both arms." And he backed up a step.

Becca swayed a moment when he let go of her, then cleared her mind and helped him back into the sling and followed him to the living room.

"Would you like me to comb out your hair? Might be kind of hard one-handed," she offered.

"That would be nice, thank you," Casey said, sitting down on one of the wooden kitchen chairs that she pulled out for him.

She combed his long black hair slowly, savoring the silkiness as she did.

"Do you want to leave it loose or tie it back or maybe put it up?" she asked.

He looked at her sideways. "You best not be suggesting a *man-bun*."

"They're very popular."

"Not with me they're not! That is the most ridiculous style I've ever seen!"

"Okay, okay. So what do you want?"

"Actually, it's been really hot. I think I'd like to get it cut. Can you do that?"

"Yes, but are you sure?" she asked. "You've always worn it long."

"Not always; in the Army, I wore it buzzcut like everyone else. I trust you, Becca." Casey smiled at her. She gulped and got a towel and some shears. A half-hour later, his hair was cut and trimmed in a pile lay on the floor. Becca ran her fingers through his hair slowly, lifting and letting it air dry. Her fingertips caressed his scalp and he closed his eyes to savor the sensation.

When she stopped, Casey ran his fingers through the layers and smiled. "You did a great job, Becca."

"I used to cut the kids' hair all the time to save money. You will likely have to have Rosa style it better when you can get over to her shop." She touched his damp hair again and he caught her fingers in his.

"I meant what I said earlier."

"I hope so." Becca gave him a shy, lopsided smile.

He leaned in closer to her and with a smile whispered, "And where's my gun? I feel half-naked without it."

"It's on the mantel behind my senior picture. I didn't want you to accidentally shoot yourself." She snickered, got him another pain pill, and while he was sleeping, she re-did his bandages that were still wet from the shower.

Thursday
5:00 pm

Jessica pulled the aging church van up near Becca's front door. Sandy started to unload their gear while Meg punched in the house security code. When it refused them entry, Meg started pounding on the door.

Becca jumped out of her chair, afraid it was David.

"Mom!" Meg called out.

Becca relaxed when she heard her daughter's familiar voice and opened the door.

"I'm so happy to see you two, but what are you doing back so soon?" Becca asked, giving each of her children a hug. "Jessica, what's wrong?"

"We need to talk," she answered. "It's ungodly hot out here, can I come in?" They all stepped inside into the cooler air of the house air conditioner.

"I'm sorry to do this, Becca, but with the lockdown, we can't get any supplies in. I managed to get some sandwich fixings from the butcher shop, but it isn't enough and I've got two dozen kids to feed. Half of them live out of town and can't go home. The only way I'm going to get through this is to take the locals back to their parents. I'm sorry," she apologized again.

"I understand, Jessica. It's okay."

"And I need a really big favor." Jessica grimaced. "Sandy and Meg both had bunkhouse mates from Dresden, another brother and sister—can those two stay here for a few days? They already know each other and it would help the church a lot. Please?"

Becca stared at the young woman. Shaking her head no, she said, "Sure."

Jessica dropped her shoulders in a visible sigh of relief and went back to the van for the other two teens.

Justin Taylor and his twin sister Tawny climbed out of the cool air of the air-conditioned van, dragging their duffle bags. Tawny was a tall yet slight girl of 17 and struggled with her heavy bag. Sandy dropped his and quickly grabbed her bag as it tumbled down the single porch step. He gave her an uncharacteristic shy smile and took both duffels into the house.

Tawny, her long chestnut hair streaked with artificial blonde and red highlights, was stronger than she let on. She had been watching Sandy for a week and now had a chance to get his attention where she had failed before. He had been too busy watching out for his sister.

Sandy dropped both bags on the floor and stared.

"Mom ... why is the sheriff here sleeping in dad's chair and wearing *my* clothes?" Sandy glared at his mother.

"We'll discuss this later, *Sanders*. Take our two guests upstairs and show them the spare rooms," Becca said through clenched teeth, glaring back. Sandy knew something serious was going on when his mother called him by his given name. "And then bring down anything that needs to be laundered." Becca walked outside with Jessica.

"Becca, why *is* the sheriff here?" Jessica whispered.

"He was shot by some kids from the campground breaking into the donut shop for food. I took him to the clinic but there isn't enough staff there to give him the temporary care he needs. At the doctor's suggestion and since we've been friends a very long time, I brought him here. We all have to pitch in and help each other during this trying time, right, Jessica?" Becca straightened her shoulders and lifted her chin to ward off any further questions, questions that might lead to confessing her previous relationship with Casey.

Jessica nodded and turned to leave.

"Jessica, wait. Please remember the ones who attacked our sheriff were from the campground and Casey is the only law left in town. Be extra careful."

ooo

Sandy came down the stairs with a basket full of clothes to be washed.

"These are Justin and Tawny's things. I figure they should be washed first since Meg and I have plenty of clean clothes in our closets," Sandy said, walking to the basement door to start the washer. He automatically took the job on since he'd been doing his own laundry after his mother returned to work when he was twelve.

"That's very thoughtful of you," his mother said gently. "I think we all need to have a talk about what's going on. When you've got the first load started, please bring everyone down here, okay?" Sandy furrowed his brow then reluctantly nodded.

ooo

"So, what did Miss Jessica tell you about the situation we're in?" Becca asked the four teenagers now sitting around the kitchen table, each with a glass of iced tea or cold water.

"Not much, Mom, just that there was some kind of toxic spill and no one could leave the town until it was cleaned up," Meg said, taking the lead.

"It's a bit more than *just* a toxic spill. The CDC is here and feels it was an act of terrorism. All the canisters in that van were intentionally opened," Casey said from the front room.

All the children looked in that direction when Becca stood and walked over to Casey.

"How are you feeling?" she asked quietly.

"Like hell," he replied. He struggled to push the foot rest down until Becca lowered it and extended her hand to help him up.

"What happened to you, Sheriff?" Sandy asked, staring at the sling he hadn't noticed before.

"I was trying to stop some vandals from breaking into a store and one of them shot me," Casey explained. "Your mom was at my office answering the phones and got me to the clinic where the doc removed the slug."

"And he's *here* because he's on painkillers and he can't stay by himself for a day or two .... Any other questions?" Becca asked, relinquishing her chair to Casey who was looking a bit unsteady on his feet.

"About a million, Ms. Burns," Justin said. "But the first ... my phone is dead. Can I use yours to call our mom? I know she's got to be worried."

"Of course, and that reminds me, everyone should get their phones or tablets on a charger," Becca suggested.

OOO

After an early yet filling dinner of cold macaroni and tuna, Casey laid down to rest and fell asleep in the chair while the two other guests went to the game room in the basement where it was even cooler.

"I still don't understand why the sheriff is *here*. Isn't there someone else that can watch over him? What is dad going to say about this?" Sandy scowled at his mother.

"Sit! Both of you!" Becca said sternly and paced a bit. "Honestly, I don't care what your father might have to say about anything. I know you both were aware that your father and I weren't getting along and I've tried to shield you from the ... unpleasantness of your father's and my relationship, but I don't think I should anymore. You are both old enough to understand what really went on." She stared up at the ceiling for a moment, taking a deep breath before going on.

"Aunt Elaine once told me to never make someone a priority in my life who considered me an option in theirs. I've been an option in David's life for a long time and I got very tired of it. Understand that although your father doesn't love me anymore, he does love the two of you. Don't ever forget that." Becca took another cleansing breath. "You know I filed for a divorce several months ago ... that was after I found out your father had another wife. Our divorce was finalized a couple of weeks ago," Becca explained.

"Wait, what other wife?" "What are you talking about?" Sandy and Meg asked at the same time.

"You heard me. While married to *me*, David married someone named Amy while he was in Las Vegas on a business trip. I have put up with his numerous affairs for over ten years, but this was the final straw. He actually thinks I didn't know about all his other women but I did, and this time, I simply could not ignore his cheating anymore! He no longer lives here, he's no longer welcome here, and he is not allowed inside this house, got it?"

Both kids were speechless.

"I had to file a restraining order to keep him away from me, and then I had all the lock codes changed to keep him from stealing things while we weren't here, which he's been doing." Becca slumped into the nearest chair. "Here are the new codes," she said, handing them each a piece of paper.

Meg swallowed hard, trying to come to grips with this new revelation. With sad eyes, she looked at her mother. "Dad told us *you* were the one having an affair. We didn't want to believe him, but Dad can be pretty convincing."

Becca sighed. "That bastard."

"I'm sorry I jumped to conclusions when I saw the sheriff here, Mom," Sandy said with a sniffle.

"Well, now that we've got that straightened out, and because David is months behind in child support, perhaps you will both understand why I've been so tight with money lately." Becca searched their faces for understanding. "I sent you two off to Camp Luna so I could pull a couple of extra shifts to catch up on the bills."

"We had no idea, Mom. I'm so sorry." Sandy stood and wrapped his long arms around his mother. "Can I ask how you found out about this Amy?"

"Would you believe she showed up here one day while you were in school? She had the nerve to demand I move out of *David's house* so she could move in."

"I remember back in February some time you were really upset and didn't want to talk about what was bothering you. You were angry and sad at the same time. It was really confusing to us. We thought it was something *we* did," Meg confessed.

"I'm sorry," Becca said. "I should have been more honest with you. I was feeling like a failure as a wife and mother."

"You've never been a failure at being our mom!" Sandy said, grinning.

OOO

"Okay, you two, time to fold your laundry," Sandy said, setting two baskets of clothes on the ping pong table, interrupting their game. They stared at him like he had two heads. "Hey, this isn't a hotel. You should feel lucky my mom is so generous to give you food, a bed, and air conditioning! So you can fold your own stuff or wear them wrinkled." He shrugged and turned away, going back upstairs to his room.

OOO

Rita Martin leaned her petite body back in her soft office chair and closed her eyes, rubbing the bridge of her nose. She'd been at the computer for eight hours, only taking short breaks to use the bathroom or drink some water. Once she even stopped for five minutes to grab a sandwich, knowing she had to eat or risk another trip to the clinic. She was close, real close to cracking into this so-called secure system; all she needed was a little more time.

Rita opened her eyes, focused, and saw the hole she was looking for. She clicked away at the keyboard for a few more minutes, grinning, and after embedding her calling card, backed out. She downloaded her route to a thumb drive and dropped it into her fireproof security box. After sending her bill and the offshore account information, she started to close the laptop and paused. All hacking job payments went off-shore; all regular computer work money went to her savings account. This job added a hefty amount to her retirement fund located in the Caymans, routed, of course, through various other banks first. She knew her way around the financial community.

Calling up a list of local banks, keeping it to within fifty miles, Rita searched for David Burns. It didn't take her long to find an account opened a year ago with only his name on it and it sported a hefty balance. David was hiding money. More importantly, he was hiding money he was supposed to have claimed in the divorce and given Becca for child support. She copied the information and pasted it to an email from a disposable account, sending it to Becca's lawyer with a simple note that would never be traced to her: "You don't know me, but I know of you. David Burns is hiding money from the court. Here is the information. Do with it what you feel is right." She hit send and closed her laptop, grinning slyly.

A glance at the clock reminded her she needed some sleep. The entire day, locked into her secure office, and with the single small window facing the backyard and blocked by the air conditioner, she never noticed all the activity across the street. She set her cell phone on the charger, and as part of her normal routine, walked through her house, checking to make sure all the doors and windows were locked. Noting how warm and humid the house was, she stretched out on the couch in her office, content to sleep in the cool room.

OOO

Cynthia Thompson turned toward the camera and pursed her red glossy lips in serious concentration.

"And now the latest breaking news on the toxic spill in Kapac. I have it from a reliable source that the CDC believes that this was not an accident and that it could very well be an act of terrorism, although no group has stepped forward to claim responsibility—yet," she said solemnly. "Virtually every canister found in the vehicle involved was opened intentionally, including one that may have contained a highly communicable virus." She turned toward the next camera on signal from the cameraman. "The CDC will begin fogging the town as soon as the proper materials and supplies are on site. Everyone is cautioned to stay indoors for 24 hours as soon as the fogging commences. Hopefully, this will be resolved soon and we can get on with Kapac Days. Flyers are available at the township hall and most local stores listing all the activities and vendors that will be in town for the festivities.

"On another note, with the latest weather shift in the area, please remember to check on your family and neighbors during this unexpected heat wave, and don't forget your pets! If you're hot, so are they."

"That's quite the breaking story, Cynthia. Congratulations on a major scoop," Don Drake said. "And the full weather report will be on right after this commercial break." Off-air, he turned to Cynthia and said, "Wow, that could really make your career. I'm impressed. Who's your reliable source?"

"Now, if I told you, it might compromise his safety." She turned away from him and sneered, knowing John Tasen was locked down in Kapac like everyone else with no way to confront her.

OOO

John Tasen and his cameraman Harry stared at the TV screen as the news turned to an ad for the local used car lot complete with a cheesy jingle.

"That was our interview!" Harry said, still staring at the screen.

"She stole my story. That bitch stole my story!" John said in disbelief. Angry, he got up and took another half sub sandwich from their in-room refrigerator, plus another beer, and sat heavy on the cheap motel chair.

OOO

Although the sun was close to setting, the air was still insufferably hot. The white sandy beach nearest the town was dotted with towels and chairs, and the water near shore was still filled with more chairs, umbrellas, and people seeking refuge from the heat. Most had not heard about the fogging and those that had didn't care. What was foremost in everyone's mind was the cool water of Luna Lake.

CHAPTER TWELVE

August 11
Friday

Becca woke slowly. The thin yellow cloth of her shorty pajama's stuck to her chest with damp sweat. With daylight streaming in through the large picture window that overlooked the peaceful backyard, she stumbled to her private bathroom and splashed some tepid water on her face. As she was drying her forehead with the fluffy green towel, she wondered why she was sweating and noticed how warm and stuffy the air was. The whole-house air conditioner had quit working.

She stripped off the damp night clothes, breathing in the heavy humid air, and let them drop to the floor, remembering Casey was on the other side of the door, sleeping and wounded. She pulled a cool, loose-fitting tank top over her head and an equally loose pair of shorts, and after sweeping her long hair up in a stylishly messy bun to keep it off her neck, she headed for the kitchen. The coffee timer she set the night before was dark; no digital clock on the stove either and nothing happened when she flipped a light switch.

The power was out.

OOO

Sandy was the first down the stairs.

"Mom, why is it so warm in here?" he asked.

"Well, the power went out sometime during the night and for some reason, the generator didn't come on. I've already called Josh and he will be over within the hour." Becca picked up a magazine and fanned herself with it. "When the others get up, take them to the basement. Even though it's 90 up here, the basement still should be ten to fifteen degrees cooler. And Sandy," she gently said to her son, "when Casey wakes, he might need help getting down the stairs."

"No worries, Mom, I'm happy to help any way I can." He was still feeling guilty that he had believed his father over his mother. His mother might have tried to shield the two of them, but she never lied to them. Sandy kissed her cheek and went in search of the battery lanterns he was sure they would need. Even though the basement was a walk-out and had a large sliding glass door that let it a great deal of daylight, it was still a basement, and three of the walls were below ground level, leaving the area in perpetual semi-darkness and always needing artificial lighting.

OOO

Becca stayed upstairs in the heat, still fanning her face with the magazine. In the one hour of the blazing morning sun cresting above the horizon, making the chemtrail streaks in the sky visible, the temperature had risen five more degrees. As soon as she saw Josh pull into the driveway in his blue and white striped work van, she stepped outside.

"Thanks so much for coming on such short notice, Josh. I can't believe how hot the house has gotten in just a few hours without the central air."

"Not a problem, Becca. I meant it when I promised I would help you out in any way I could. Now, this generator is a whole-house unit, right? And it's set to come on when the power has been interrupted for five minutes?" Josh refreshed his memory while they walked around the side of the house and down the shaded slope toward the large generator where it sat next to the walk-out basement doors. "Remind me what the fuel source is."

"It's on propane, and before you ask, I had the tank refilled two weeks ago," Becca answered, struggling to breathe the hot, moist air.

Josh nodded silently, checked the tank level anyway, and then removed the computerized gas sniffer from his tool kit, letting it boot up to test the lines. He passed it over each connection, frowned, and passed it over a valve a second time; it should have given off a minute reading. Grabbing hold of the valve, he gave it a twist and shook his head.

A few moments later, Becca heard the generator spring to life and, startled, looked over to Josh.

"Someone turned the propane feed off, that's all." Josh smiled. "Likely the propane company did it as a safety procedure while they were filling the tank and they forgot to turn it back on. You shouldn't have any more problems, but if you do, call me."

"Wow, that was so easy! What do I owe you for the house call?" she asked.

"Nothing."

"I know your time is valuable, Josh."

"Tell you what, after all this settles down, let me take you out to dinner." He smiled shyly at her, hoping she couldn't hear his heart galloping in his chest.

"You mean, like a *date*? I don't think so, Josh. I've only been divorced for a couple of weeks and I'm not ready to start *dating*." Her mind instantly returned her to Casey's kiss the day before and she felt like a hypocrite.

"Oh, just a casual thing, maybe for a pizza, ya know, as old friends?" The panicked look in her eyes told him to back off or she might stop talking to him and he'd lose her all over again. "Just friends," he repeated.

"Oh, well, that's different." She breathed a sigh of relief, still feeling guilty. "Let's talk about it another time then, okay?"

He didn't push the issue, because he knew she'd be calling him again real soon. Becca might have power for the air conditioner and the appliances, but he already knew the entire town was out, and that meant the city well pumps and the pumps for the sewer lift stations were out too. Everyone was dependent on the city for water. It was one of those sad facts of life when people gave control to the government in exchange for a convenience. He'd get to see her again when she called him to fix her water. Josh was very patient.

OOO

Becca walked up the slope with Josh and thanked him again for coming over so quickly. Out of breath from the heat, she let herself in the front door and engaged the locks and the alarm, pushing Josh's surprising offer to the back of her mind. She put her hand over the nearest vent and felt the cool air pulsing through. It would take a while before they really felt a return of more comfortable temperatures and she descended into the cool basement.

"We've got generator power on now," Becca announced, "though it will take an hour or two for the a/c to cool off the entire house. Then we'll be back to normal, or as normal as we can be under the circumstances."

OOO

Even though the central air conditioner would eventually cool and dehumidify the house, Becca brought two fans in from the garage to help while she made pancakes for breakfast. She had four teens and a man to feed, and she doubted their appetites would wait.

OOO

Rita woke with a kink in her neck from sleeping on the couch, and quickly noticed how warm the room was. The lights that normally came from her desktop computer were out, as was the blinking light from her cellphone charger.

"Well, crap," Rita mumbled. She moved to her bedroom and pulled out something cool to wear, laying it across the still-made bed. She turned on the shower faucet and sighed when nothing happened.

In the kitchen, she opened the fridge, grabbed a bottle of water, and quickly closed that door to keep any residual coolness inside. Back in the bathroom, she opened the bottle of water and after taking a long drink, poured the rest into the sink after closing the trap. With a wash cloth, she took what her mother always called a PTA-bath—Pits, Tits, and Ass—and after splashing her face got dressed in shorts and a loose sleeveless blouse. The day was already promising to be brutally hot. Again.

Rita sat in her office and thought about what to do next. Even though her geek brain seemed to focus in a different, more gadget-oriented direction, she was still a very practical person and that practical side reminded her that her equipment and files were very sensitive on multiple levels and must be protected. Rita emptied a few things out of her large purse and put her sleek laptop in. Next, she dumped the contents of the larger fireproof box into a plastic baggie and stuck that in her purse too. The thumb drives would not be damaged in any way from being loose, but she didn't want to risk that they could be corrupted from the increased heat. She grabbed her insulin kit from the refrigerator, plus the refill she got the other day, the phone off the charger, and then headed across the street.

OOO

Rita felt a waft of cool air when Becca opened the door. "Thank you, Aunt Elaine!" she said, closing her eyes and smiling. "I can feel you're not affected by the power outage."

"But I am. The house is on the generator," Becca replied.

"Oh. Wait, I hear water running." Rita looked confused.

"Sandy is upstairs taking a shower. Come on in, Rita. You want coffee or iced tea?"

"I'll take the iced tea," Rita answered. "And how is it you have water? Mine is out."

"Another thing to thank Aunt Elaine for: she insisted on not hooking up to the city for water or sewage until absolutely necessary. We're still on a well and septic, and that well pump is now powered by the generator and the septic doesn't require power, just gravity."

"You might be the only one in the entire town that has water," Rita murmured.

"I know, and it's a good thing the house sits this far back from the road or as quiet as it is, the neighbors might hear the generator. But hey, these power outages never last very long." Becca shrugged. She looked at Rita's large purse. "Are you moving in for a few days?"

Rita looked sheepish. "Yeah, at least until the power comes back—if you don't mind."

"Of course I don't mind, though you need to know a few things ..."

"Like what? Please don't tell me David is here."

"Good Lord, no! But the kids are back from camp along with their bunkmates, so there are four teens upstairs, and Casey's here, too."

"Whoa, slow down! Casey moved in? You moved on fast, Becca. Good for you!" Rita gave her a high-five.

"No, no, Casey didn't move in! Casey was shot a few days ago, and he's been staying here while he recovers. That's all."

Rita was stunned. "What happened?"

Becca related all the details she could, as quickly as she could. "He will likely be going back to the office today or tomorrow. There's nothing going on between us." She hated lying to her best friend, but she wasn't sure there *was* anything developing—or redeveloping—with the sheriff.

"Are you sure?" Rita smirked. "You two were pretty tight in high school."

"Let's get back to practical matters. You need a room." Becca called down the basement stairs, "Meg, Tawny, can you please come up here?"

○○○

"Tawny, this is my best friend, Rita. She's going to be staying here while the power is out. Consequently, Meg, since your room is the only one with two single beds, Tawny will have to move in with you and Rita will take Tawny's room," Becca explained the new arrangement.

"No problem, Mom. Tawny and I shared a room for almost a week. We'll go shift things now, and I'll put the sheets on to wash after I put fresh ones on the bed," Meg offered.

"I need to get a few things from home," Rita said. "And everything from my refrigerator and freezer should come too."

"With what happened to Casey, I'll send both boys with you. Even though that incident was centered on stores with food, we can't be too cautious."

"Okay, great. By the way, Becca, where *is* Casey?" Rita whispered.

"With the kids going up and down the stairs. He couldn't sleep in the recliner—*like he's been doing, Rita*—so he's napping in my room."

○○○

Sandy and Justin carried the cooler between them, and Rita followed with a small wheeled suitcase filled with clothes and her device chargers.

"Sorry, there's not a lot of food. I've been too busy to do any shopping, and I usually call for a pizza or stop for some take-out for dinner," Rita apologized to Becca. They loaded the items into the fridge and put the cooler in the garage out of the way.

"Don't worry about it. I still have plenty on the shelf after resupplying from David's pilfering of my pantry."

○○○

Friday
Noon

John and Margi Maguire set out six solar-powered battery lanterns on the breakfast dining table. "Once the sun goes down tonight, it will get really dark in here without power, so we have a safe solar-charged battery lantern for each room," he explained to their B&B guests. "I'm going to line them up on the table in the back to make sure they are fully charged. When you come back in from whatever you're doing today, don't forget to take one back to your room, and then put them out again in the morning. Hopefully by then, though, the power should be back on."

"Sure glad I picked these up when I did. I should have gotten more though. I'll put that on the next shopping list," John said to his wife after everyone had left for the day.

"That takes care of the guests. Now, what about us?" Margi asked.

"We have all those oil lamps you've collected over the years. I don't trust the guests to use those safely, but I do trust us. Now let's get them washed and ready."

"Do we have enough fuel?"

"There is a full five-gallon can of kerosene in the shed— it's the blue one next to the red ones with regular gas for the mower. If you want to start washing the globes, I'll take the bases out to the picnic table to fill."

When Margi turned on the kitchen faucet to wash the globes, she was reminded they didn't have water. She followed John out to the shed, grabbed a bucket, and filled it from the lake. After washing and drying the globes, she had a thought.

"John, just in case we need water later for flushing, I think we should put a bucket of lake water in every bathroom. We can always dump it down the sink if the power comes back."

OOO

Carl Linden quietly opened the door of his apartment and let himself back into his grocery store. As dark as the place was, without lights and the window shades pulled down tight, he still knew his way around the aisles. When the power went out overnight, he realized he had only one flashlight and the batteries it held were about dead. He needed more and knew right where they were.

He'd brought one of his sturdy cloth bags and took all the D-cell and all the C-cell batteries on the spinning rack. Those would power his flashlights and his small battery fan. Below that was a shelf with the AA and the AAA batteries, and not remembering what he had that took what, all of those too went into his bag along with two new lanterns. He might not have power to watch TV, but he would have light to read by, and that was his preferred past time anyway.

Carl went back up the stairs and once again locked the door behind him.

OOO

1:00 pm

Lisa Eddington wandered through her apartment, closing drapes and pulling down blinds, the bright sun already heating up the shop. She got a bottle of water from the now warm refrigerator and drank half of it. As she looked out over the lake, it occurred to her she hadn't seen Mrs. Ostrander all morning.

She walked across the hot, sticky sand, trying to stay in the limited shade, and made her way up the wooden steps to the old lady's back door. The short walk in the intense heat nearly wore her out and she was glad Agnes was staying indoors.

Tapping lightly, she called out, "Mrs. O? Agnes? Are you here? Is everything alright?" With no answer, Lisa turned the doorknob and finding it unlocked, opened the door. "Agnes?" The air inside was hot, stale and ... sour. "Agnes?" she called out again. Stepping into the kitchen, she saw the elderly woman with her head down on the small table.

Lisa walked up to her and as soon as she touched the purple gingham sleeve, she saw the dark red blood pooling under Agnes' head. She yanked her hand away and backed up. Pulling the phone from her pocket, she quickly dialed 911 and got a rapid busy signal. Emergency services were out.

Lisa went back to her house, grabbed her keys, and drove over to the sheriff's office, only to find it locked. Not knowing what else to do, she went to the emergency clinic.

Dr. Jones had his head down on the desk, much like Agnes, only when Lisa touched his arm, he sat up startled.

"Sorry, it's been a rough night," he mumbled. "What can I do for you? Lisa, right?"

"Yeah, Lisa Eddington. I called 911 but no one answered, and the sheriff's office is locked, and I think Mrs. Ostrander, the old lady next door to me, is dead," Lisa said, sniffing.

"What makes you think she's dead?" Dr. Jones asked, now fully alert.

"Her head is lying in a pool of blood?"

"Shit!" he said.

"Yeah, there's that too." Lisa frowned. "Do you know where the sheriff is?"

"As a matter of fact, I do," the doctor answered. "I should check Mrs. Ostrander first."

OOO

Dr. Jones tentatively tapped on Becca's door, not sure if they were even there.

Rita peeked through the small window, and recognizing her doctor, opened the door.

"Rita? I thought Becca Burns lived here," he said confused, a smile still reaching his eyes at seeing her.

"Oh, she does. I live across the street," she answered. "Do you need to see her?"

"Actually, I need to talk with the sheriff. Is he here?"

"Sure is. Come on in and have a seat. I'll find him." Rita closed and locked the door once the doctor and a vaguely familiar woman were inside. She eyed the woman and wondered if this was the doctor's girlfriend. That would explain why he rejected her clumsy advances.

OOO

"Are you sure you feel up to going to the office, Casey?" Becca asked, concentrating on buttoning his shirt and avoiding his eyes. She had managed to get most of the blood out

105

of his tan uniform shirt but couldn't do anything about the missing sleeve, so she had cut the other one and hemmed them both to at least be even.

"I will admit my arm is sore and a bit stiff, but it's much better than it was, and I can't avoid what's going on any longer." He slipped his finger under her chin to tilt her head up to meet his eyes. "And if it's okay, I'll come back here later."

They were interrupted by Rita knocking on and opening the door to Becca's bedroom as Becca resumed adjusting Casey's sling.

"Hey," Rita said, "Micah Jones is here and needs to talk with you, Casey."

OOO

"I think we have a homicide on our hands, Sheriff," the doctor said. "And while I'm here, I should take a look at your arm."

"The arm is doing better. Becca has kept it clean and changed the bandage twice a day. Oh, and the pain itself is down to a minimum. My last pain pill was twelve hours ago and I'm doing fine," Casey said. "So, what makes you think we have a homicide?"

"Can we talk privately?"

While the two men discussed what the doctor had found, Becca, Rita, and Lisa stepped into the kitchen.

"You're Becca Burns?" Lisa asked quietly. "Are you any relation to David?"

"David is my ex-husband, why?" Becca frowned.

"Oh, ex-husband, that's a relief." Lisa looked relieved at the news.

"Why is that?"

"Because David and I have been sort of dating for the last several months, and I was getting the feeling he wasn't telling me everything," Lisa explained.

Becca started to laugh and Rita snickered.

"Why is that funny?" Lisa asked guardedly.

"I'm sorry for laughing, Lisa. David and I have been divorced for all of three weeks, because about ten months ago, he married someone else. He's a real piece of work."

"Wait a minute. Are you saying he married someone while still married to you and then he started dating *me*, all at the same time?"

"That pretty much sums up David," Rita finally injected, snickering.

"But ..." Lisa looked scared and mumbled something ever so quietly to herself.

"Becca," Casey called into the kitchen. "I'm going to catch a ride with these two and pick up my squad car, then check out this death."

ooo

"I didn't touch anything except to check for a pulse," Dr. Jones said. The three of them stood in Mrs. Ostrander's kitchen, the body in the same position as when Lisa found her. Casey looked over at Lisa.

"I had just touched her sleeve when I noticed the blood, then I backed away," she answered his unasked question.

"Lisa, you might want to wait outside," the sheriff said. "Better yet, why don't you go on home? And thank you for checking on her like you did. She could have sat here for days if you hadn't."

After she left, the sheriff gently lifted the old woman's head, exposing the neck for the doctor to examine.

"One clean slice. She probably bled out within minutes." He pushed back some of her steel gray hair. "And check this out—there's a large contusion on her right temple."

"So, someone hit her in the head, likely from behind, which would make our assailant right-handed, and knocked her unconscious, and then sliced her throat to kill her. So someone wanted to make sure she was dead, not just injured and not putting up a fight," Casey thought out loud. "A knife is usually the weapon of a woman, but a man will use anything."

"Without power, there isn't any place to put her," Dr. Jones said, reminding Casey of their dire situation.

"Oh there is: Johnson's Funeral Home. The back half of the building is the morgue. I'm surprised you didn't know that, Doctor."

"I've only been here a few months and haven't needed those ... services before today," the doctor confessed.

The sheriff grabbed a colorful afghan off the nearby couch and covered the body. "I'll stop over there and talk with Mr. Johnson about storing the body."

"Where are your deputies, Sheriff?" the doctor asked as they descended the creaky old steps and walked around the front to Casey's squad car.

Casey sighed, wondering how many more times he would have to explain his deputies' absence.

"They're brothers and I had to give them both the weekend off when their father passed away suddenly. Now they can't get back into Kapac, like so many others."

"Are you sure your arm is okay? You look a little pale."

"I'm fine, Doc, really, just a little sore and tired. You ever try sleeping in a chair with four teenagers in the house?" he asked, chuckling.

"At least you've got power and a/c. This heat is brutal." He looked up at the sky. "Looks like we might get more rain, which would be good if it cools things off a bit." He took a deep breath and wrinkled his nose. "I also noticed on the drive to pick you up that people were putting their trash cans out."

"Friday has always been garbage day for as long as I remember." Casey stopped walking. "There are no municipal trucks that are stationed here in town. This is going to be a real smelly problem in a few days. And not just the smell—it could bring in the wolves and coyotes, too."

"And rats," the doc added, once again reminded of his time in Chicago.

OOO

"Sandy, Casey called and said there wouldn't be any trash collection today. Would you and Justin bring the trash cans back into the garage? I doubt there will be any pick up at all until the town is open again. And move my car out so it doesn't get stinky," Becca said, tossing Sandy her car keys.

"You seem to get along really well with your mom," Justin said to Sandy once they were in the garage.

"Yeah, the three of us have always been pretty tight. She's one of those parents who doesn't jump to conclusions, and she has always been there for us, no matter what. I remember having an English Lit teacher who was really hard on me because I disagreed with her on the interpretation of a story—Mom stuck up for me."

"Lucky you."

"Yeah, I guess I am pretty lucky," Sandy agreed and silently vowed to be more like his mom and not jump to conclusions or make snap judgments anymore.

OOO

"Mr. Johnson, this is Sheriff WhiteCloud. I need to talk to you. I'm on my way now," Casey said after his call was answered.

"Of course, Sheriff. Come around to the morgue entrance," Johnson said in his quiet, soothing voice.

After unlocking the morgue double delivery doors, Mr. Johnson led the sheriff to his neat office located near the front of the funeral home. Casey immediately noticed it was air-conditioned and that the lights were on in the morgue exam room.

"I'm glad to see you have power, sir. I'm going to need your services. I just came from a murder scene," Casey explained.

"Who is the deceased?"

"Agnes Ostrander. Do you know her?

"Ah, a nice lady and a wise woman. She had come by early in the summer to make—and pay for—her final arrangements. Too many people wait until they can't make their wishes known, leaving the difficult decisions up to their grieving loved ones after they have passed."

"Can you pick up the body and store it here in the freezer?" Casey came right to the point.

"Of course, Sheriff. Joe Jr. and I will see to it immediately." He stood and walked Casey back to the doors.

"I'm assuming you are on a generator, Mr. Johnson," Casey said.

"Considering the fragile nature of my ... clients, it would be very foolish to not have all contingencies covered."

Friday night
11:00 pm

The semi pulled slowly into the dark and quiet town. The driver parked the rig next to Grayson Park and silently emerged from the cab. Letting down the stabilizer legs of the plain white, unmarked trailer, he disengaged it from the tractor. After unlocking the rear doors, and leaving them closed, he got back into the tractor, made a U-turn, and headed back to the military barricade.

CHAPTER THIRTEEN

August 12
Saturday morning
8:00 am

Casey WhiteCloud emerged from the back office where he had slept on a cot. It was minimally more comfortable than the recliner, but definitely quieter. He pulled off the white T-shirt he had slept in and was in process of buttoning one of the half-dozen short-sleeved shirts that were always in the office closet, when he noticed the semi-trailer parked a half block down on the other side of the street. What alarmed him was it was cab-less. The suspicion of terrorists immediately jumped out at him. The biggest question on his mind though was how did they get past the roadblock? And if someone could get in, perhaps they were going to get out soon. He had been out of commission for a few days but now needed to check in at the roadblock.

He put his wide-brimmed hat on to keep the already scorching sun off his neck, checked his weapon, and stepped out into the street.

Casey cautiously walked completely around the trailer, giving it a thirty-foot berth, noting it had no markings of any kind, and then almost tiptoed to the massive rear doors. With weapon drawn after noticing the doors unlocked, he edged one open. To his surprise, the trailer was filled with cases of bottled water. A town without power was a town without water, and now that problem was solved. He flung both doors completely open and smiled as he wondered who to thank.

After delivering six cases of water to the clinic and having the doc change his bandage, Casey drove through the subdivisions, starting at the back, and used his loud speaker to announce there would be cases of water given away at Grayson Park at 10:00 am.

At 9:30 am, a crowd had formed, all thirsty and all anxious to get their share.

"Jonah, would you and Frank help with distributing?" Casey asked two of the younger, more fit-looking men. "If one of you stays up in the trailer and keeps piling the cases on the edge, the other can hand them out."

Casey climbed up into the trailer to address the crowd. "Before we start handing out the water, I want everyone here to know, and please spread the word, that I don't know much more about what's going on than you do. I was at the scene, and I do know there was a possible major accident involving hazardous material. After that, we were shut down and I was shut out of any further information.

"All of the city officials were out of town at the time and now can't get back in. All of our volunteer firefighters seem to be missing too. I'm still trying to get more information about that. When I do, I will call for another town meeting here in the park. Also, because of the situation, there are no city services available—you already know that means no running water and no sanitation, so that also means no garbage pickup. So anyone who has put their trash out, take it back in and secure it in your garage or a shed until this situation ends or else it will be a real mess for *you* to clean up if the dogs get into it.

"And as of right now, I'm instituting a dark to dawn curfew. Hopefully, that will keep everyone a bit safer while I try to find out what's going on."

"Sheriff, before the shutdown, I heard a couple of the firemen saying they were taking the main pumper truck and the EMS ambulance into Appleton for tune-ups and to wash and wax them to spiff them up for the Kapac Days parade," Frank said.

"Thanks for the info, Frank. I can stop looking for them now." Casey sighed. "Other than that, people, I have no answers for you. Without knowing when this will end, you need to ration whatever food you have. We *will* get through this as long as we keep our heads and help each other out.

"I don't know how much is here, so there will be one case per person until we run out. Remember, there is a hand pump at the campground as an alternative if there aren't enough cases to go around or for when you run out, so hold onto your empties. Keep it civil, everyone!" Then he got down.

Inside of twenty minutes, there was shoving, shouting, and a few punches thrown when the line didn't move fast enough for some. Tempers rose as the temperature did. Those next in line to getting their water grabbed two cases and ran, only to be tackled and their water taken by someone not willing to wait, leaving them with nothing.

Casey stepped between the crowd and the trailer and was immediately pushed aside. Someone pushed another and that one bumped into someone else and that one tripped Casey. He landed on his left side and grimaced. The stitches in his arm ripped, sending a fresh stream of blood running down to his fingers.

"Damn!" he muttered. "Jonah, Frank, take your cases and let this mob get their own." He was getting disgusted with the growing lack of self-control in the town people.

OOO

"You're getting to be a regular here, Sheriff," Dr. Micah Jones commented.

"Since I am, you might as well start calling me Casey." He stuck his hand out to the doctor.

The doctor grinned and took the offered hand. "Micah."

After getting his arm re-stitched, Casey locked the door to his office and stretched out on the cot. It was a few minutes past noon.

OOO

"Becca, hi," Josh said.

"Is there something wrong, Josh?" Becca asked with a concerned frown.

"Not really. With the entire town being without power *and* water, I thought I would bring you some. I've been over to the campground to get water for myself from their hand-pump. It might be the only place to get clean drinking water," he announced, setting down a large, blue five-gallon plastic container on her porch.

"I appreciate the thought, Josh, but I've got water. The only thing my aunt hooked up to when the subdivision went in was the new underground powerlines. Even though the water and sewage lines were brought up to the house by the contractor, I'm still on a well *and* a septic. I thought you knew that," Becca replied with a grateful smile. "Why don't you keep that and save yourself a trip tomorrow?"

"I forgot. I'm really happy you've got things so in control here. Like I've said before, if there's anything you need, just call." Josh went back to his van, his face flaming from embarrassment and hurt that she didn't need him like he thought she would.

OOO

The pounding on the outer office door woke the sheriff from a troubled sleep. He staggered to the door, cradling his freshly wounded arm, thinking at this rate, his arm would never heal.

"What's up, Frank?" he asked, disengaging the lock.

"As I was going home with my water, Sheriff, I passed by Mr. Alder's house and realized I hadn't seen him at the water giveaway. So I stopped in." He frowned and took a deep breath. "You need to come with me, Sheriff. I think he's dead."

Frank pushed the front door open. The small bungalow was dark. A sliver of light from the persistent sun leaked in at the bottom of the shades being pulled tight against the heat, but it was still hot inside, which increased the rancid odors.

"Where is he?" Casey asked.

Frank pointed to the closed door that led to the kitchen and then stepped aside. "If you don't mind, Sheriff, I really don't want to go in there again."

Casey nodded and opened the door, then quickly closed it again. The smell was ten times worse in the closed-up room. He pulled a cloth handkerchief from his pocket and covered his nose and mouth, then stepped back inside.

Old Mr. Adler sat at his kitchen table, head resting on his folded arms. There wasn't any obvious blood this time; the old man's dog had licked it all up and lay snoozing at his master's feet, its muzzle covered in dried and caked blood.

Casey was thankful he hadn't had lunch yet.

OOO

"Dr. Jones, come with me. We have another victim. Mr. Johnson will meet us there with the hearse."

OOO

Becca looked out the small window in the door and opened it wide when she saw Casey.

"I thought you were coming back last night," she said. Her expression completely changed when she saw how distressed he was. "What's happened, Casey?"

"I've just come from the second homicide," he told her. "We have a serial killer in town. I need to talk to everyone here, and *now*."

Becca ushered the four teens into the big kitchen and had them sit at the large wooden table. Earlier, she and Rita had put the extension leaf in to accommodate the six of them; seven when Casey was there. Rita also sat, Becca elected to stand, and Casey refused to sit.

"I'm not going into any details, because for the most part they're irrelevant. However, there have been two murders in town in the last two days. Because the details are so similar, I'm confident it's the same killer."

"A serial killer?" Justin gasped.

"Yes, Justin, that's exactly what I think. Therefore, with Becca's permission, I'm making a few strong, very strong, suggestions while you are here.

"First, no one is ever alone. No one goes outside alone, and no one even goes to the basement alone. The doors remain locked at all times. Rita, if you need to go to your house for whatever reason, do *not* go by yourself.

"Second, when everyone is in the house, do not, I repeat, do *not* open the door. Unless it's me or you trust them. Understood?"

"What if it's my dad?" Meg asked.

"Honestly, Meg, your father is not supposed to be coming here for any reason, so no, not even for your dad because *I* don't trust him," Becca answered, backing up Casey's new rules.

"I'm going back to my office for a few hours, and I'll be back around 6:00 pm," Casey said to Becca. "You've got my cell number. Don't hesitate to call if you need me back sooner."

ooo

When Casey pulled up in front of his office, he found Micah pacing the sidewalk.

"Where have you been?" Micah nearly shouted.

"Please don't tell me what I think you're going to tell me," Casey said sadly.

"Another woman, younger this time though, and she was strangled."

ooo

Inside the rental house two doors down from the clinic, a very distraught husband sat in the living room, alternating between clenching his hands together and softly sobbing.

Casey sat on a chair across from the man and gently questioned him. "Where were you when this happened, Mr. Opat?"

"I was out looking for food. Karen was getting really hungry. I was gone maybe an hour."

"Why that long?"

"I was walking. The car is out of gas because we've been running it for the air conditioning every few hours. I happened to go by the sub shop when I noticed a broken window and someone inside sweeping up the glass, so I stopped in. The young girl was really nice and made me up a couple of sandwiches—for free. I got Karen a salami and cheese with lettuce, her favorite ..." his voice hitched and he sobbed again. "When I got back, I found her in the kitchen. I thought she was sleeping."

Casey and Micah went into the small kitchen, leaving the husband sitting on the couch. A young woman of about thirty sat at the small table, head resting on her folded arms. There was no blood; she had been strangled with an extension cord that still dangled around her neck. Micah brushed her red hair aside and Casey immediately saw the beginning of a bruise on her right temple.

"With the exception of the cause of death being strangulation, the MO and the staging is the same. This is number three," Casey said sadly. "I'm ruling out the husband. Unless he killed the other two, he wouldn't know about these details, and his alibi will be easy enough to check out with Cathy at the sub shop. I'll call Mr. Johnson. Maybe I should put him on speed dial."

"Why would the killer chose a different weapon this time?" Micah asked.

"A very sharp knife, like what's been used with the other two, is fast and efficient. Strangling is more personal because it takes longer and the victim suffers more. The killer's violence level is escalating."

Casey stared at the ceiling for a long thoughtful moment. He pushed the possibilities to the back of his mind temporarily. "I'd like to check his alibi with Cathy at the sub shop and see if they need any help boarding up the window."

After Mr. Johnson left with the latest victim, Casey sat down across the husband.

"I'm so very sorry for your loss, sir. I *will* find out who did this. Will you be okay for now?" With a solemn nod of his head in response, Casey and Micah left.

On the walk back to the clinic, Casey said, "That bruise on her head looked so minor. It didn't look like it could knock her out."

"It would have turned into a real doozy, but once the heart stops beating, there's no blood getting to injuries, and that's what a bruise is: blood trying to heal a wound," Micah explained.

OOO

"Thanks for asking, Sheriff, but Dad had some plywood out back that he was going to use for making a display," Cathy explained when Casey commented on the wood-covered windows.

"Was anything missing when you discovered the damage?"

"Nothing more than a few bags of potato chips—everything else is put away nightly. I consider us pretty lucky."

CHAPTER FOURTEEN

Saturday
4:00 pm

"Miss Eddington? Lisa?" Micah Jones called out. The front door to the gift shop stood ajar, letting more hot air into the already over-heated building. The doctor pushed it further with the case of water he was carrying. "Are you here? Your door is open, and that's not very safe right now." Antiques and knick-knacks of every nature and size filled every space available on the dozens of tables he passed as he edged closer to the back where he assumed the private residence was. "I brought you a case of water. Lisa?" He stepped into the empty kitchen and set the water down beside a note that was propped up on the table. He picked it up and read:

> I don't have any other choice. I'm pregnant with David Burns' child and I know now we have no future. I tried to call him, but he hung up on me and now my calls go straight to his voicemail. Agnes was right that he would bring me nothing but grief. I can't bring a child into the world like this.
>
> I'm sorry to whoever finds me.
>
> Lisa

Dr. Jones dropped the note and quickly went through the entire apartment. Maybe he wasn't too late; maybe he could save her. He found her in the bathtub, and he knew he was too late.

OOO

Casey heard the pounding on Becca's front door and looked out the window at Micah. "Please don't tell me we have another murder," he said to the doctor. Lightning flashed behind him as the sky opened up with more hot rain.

"No, not a murder," he replied quietly. "A suicide: Lisa Eddington."

"*What?*"

"Is there anything to drink here? I sure could use something strong."

Becca came down the stairs from talking with Rita when she heard the knocking on the door. She looked at the doctor then back at Casey. "What's going on?"

"Do you have anything stronger than wine in the house?" Casey asked gently.

"Sure, bourbon, scotch, or brandy?" she offered, not liking the looks on their faces. "I'll get all three." Becca retrieved the bottles from a cupboard and set them on the kitchen table where the two men now sat. She got two short glasses and filled them with ice. Then she sat.

"Tell me what's going on," she said with a scowl.

Micah poured some bourbon and downed it in one gulp, then poured more, wiped his hand over his face, and handed Casey the suicide note.

After reading it, Casey poured a small amount of brandy and said to Becca, "I hate David." He drank the brandy and set the glass aside.

Becca gently removed the note from Casey's anger-clenched fingers. She took a couple of deep breaths to tamp down a sob after reading the note. "That poor girl." She looked at the doctor and asked, "How?"

"She sat in the bathtub and slit her wrists, and then she drove the knife into her belly," Micah answered, leaning back in the chair and sighing. He stared at the ceiling for a while and frowned, trying hard to control his own emotions. He had seen more death in the past few days than he had in the past year, even in Chicago. Lisa's death hit him the hardest, maybe because she was pregnant.

"I hope the two of you don't think badly of me for this, but I'm not going back to the clinic," Dr. Micah Jones said. "I just can't do it anymore. That building is so damn hot I can barely breathe! Like most hospitals, where there are windows, those windows don't open. Without power, it's also so dark I have to see people in the lobby where there is sunlight.

"Besides, I'm only one man and the only ones coming in now are the elderly with signs of heatstroke. I give them a bottle of water and tell them to stay in the shade out of the sun or stay indoors and most importantly to reduce their activity. They don't listen—they want a pill to make it go away and refuse to take responsibility.

"And then there are the kids that have been in fights. It's mostly scratches, but they've been so coddled their entire lives they think they're mortally wounded. It's only been two days since the power went out and without their damn cell phones, they're bored, lost. They have spent so much time texting they're addicted, and now they don't know what to do with themselves. Have you ever watched them—I mean really watched them? They walk like zombies, their focus on those damn phones in their hands. That's another batch refusing to take personal responsibility: they walk right into the street without looking, expecting drivers to stop for them. Do you realize that more than half of the 13–18 year olds don't even know how to use a manual can opener? Or how to do their own laundry? Mindless idiots, all of them!"

"I certainly don't blame you, Micah. We've been in lockdown for one week—that's it, *one week*—and I've watched the town disintegrate. And like you, I'm only one man. I've been shot, knocked down, kicked, and the worst? I've been ignored," Casey said.

"What are you two going to do? No one can leave Kapac," Becca said, looking back and forth between the two men at her table. She suddenly felt vindicated from the guilt that she had taught her kids basic cooking and how to do their own laundry when they were young, as minor as that seemed in the scope of everything else.

Casey looked into her chocolate eyes, smiled, and took her hand, not caring that the doctor saw. "This might put you under a great deal of stress, Becca, but I'm going to ask you to let me move in, temporarily. You have the safest and, quite frankly, the most comfortable situation right here, and if this lasts much longer, I think you're going to need the extra security."

"You really think we might be in danger?" Becca asked, wide-eyed.

"Maybe not immediately, but you have power and water *and* food, something the rest of the town is fighting over right now. Besides, if I'm not at my peak, I can't help the town, and my office is just as suffocating as the clinic."

"Can I stay too, until I figure out something else?" Micah asked.

Becca sat speechless and bewildered, then nodded her agreement.

"Doc, we need to secure the clinic. From what I understand, the upper levels are accessible only by the stairs right now without power for the elevator, right? So if we can lock those stairwells, they should be safe from vandals."

"I guess. I'm a doctor; I don't know anything about the functioning of the building. I do know that all the exterior windows are bullet or shatter-proof and the same for the pharmacy," Micah answered. "Oh, when I left, I did lock the emergency room doors. Will that be enough?"

"It might be. However, we still need to check it out. Some of those kids might start looking for drugs and we have to make sure they can't get to any. You have any personal stuff there that you might need?" Casey asked. "I've got a few things at my office I'll want to get." He turned to Becca and said, "We will also try to get extra supplies. I know you said you had about a month of food on hand, but that was for the three of you. There will now be eight to feed and that will drastically deplete your supply and quickly."

"I'll talk to the kids about rationing, and Rita did bring over everything she had in the fridge and freezer," Becca said. "How long will you two be gone?"

"I don't know. With this rain, though, everyone should be inside, so we shouldn't have any delays." Unconcerned about the doctor, Casey brushed his lips across Becca's and left.

OOO

Becca stood at the glass door leading out to the upper deck where the grill sat. No matter how many times it rained, the ground was still parched, as if for some reason the rain wasn't soaking in. The current rain pounded the dry yard, sending muddy rivulets coursing through the uneven back acreage. She was feeling more than a bit overwhelmed by everything that had happened over the last week. With the kids at the church retreat, she had been alone in the big house, but now there would be eight of them. Her breath caught in her chest when she thought of the implications and the possibilities all of that meant. And she thought about Casey. His touch was gentle and his kisses were warm with promise; that was something she hadn't gotten from her husband in too many years. *My ex-husband*, she reminded herself. As she stood there, she heard the muted sounds of a jet flying overhead, high above clouds and she wondered...

Pulling away from her reverie, Becca knew each one in the house would depend on her for something, one way or another, and as much as the thought terrified her, being needed also warmed her and gave her purpose.

She scrubbed a half-dozen potatoes, carrots, celery, and onions. Realizing all that might not go far enough, Becca put three of the potatoes back in the fridge to use with another meal and got out a bag of rice. After cutting everything into smaller pieces than she normally would she set them into the roasting pan with the pot roast that was already cooking in the oven. Then she got out a big pot to cook the rice in. Her mind ran through the various things she would have to adjust to make the food go further and she cut the pot roast into stew-sized pieces—and gravy; she would have to make more gravy.

With dinner all set, Becca went back upstairs to talk with Rita.

"More changes, Rita," she said.

"Now what?" Rita casually closed her laptop. There was no one she trusted more than Becca, but even that trust had a limit.

"Dr. Micah is moving in here for a few days."

"Well, shit! Are you opening a boarding house?" Rita snickered. "And where is he going to sleep?" Rita felt a warm glow, and selfish relief, that Micah would be nearby. She was feeling better, yet not 100% herself.

"We haven't figured that part out yet, though I'm thinking in the basement. It's cooler and quieter. In fact, it might be good for Casey to move down there too," Becca added.

"Why isn't Casey moving into your room?" Rita casually leaned back in the hard wooden chair and almost toppled over. Becca snickered as she grabbed the arm of the chair to steady it.

Becca sat down on the small twin bed and faced her best friend. "I will admit that my previous feelings for Casey are ... re-immerging, and I think his are too, but we're not there yet, Rita, okay? I, for one, don't want to rush into anything."

"Okay, I'll back off," Rita said, "but I still think you two would make a dynamite couple!"

"In time, maybe. Come on downstairs. There's something you need to read," Becca said. Once in the kitchen, she handed Rita Lisa's note.

"Well, double shit!" She dropped the note on the table.

"I know. Now, back to another issue: food. I know you brought over everything perishable, but is there anything else you still have over there? Maybe like pasta or rice or soup?"

"I do! Let me shut down my program and I'll be right down."

"What are you working on?"

"Just stuff," Rita said, side-stepping the question. Upstairs, she hit send to deliver the second notice to the agency that had contracted her services. A second notice was never necessary before and it angered her. She jogged down the steps two at a time to catch up to Becca.

By the time Rita got back to the kitchen, Becca had gotten both boys away from their ping pong game and ready to go with her.

"I know it's only across the street, Mom, but it's pouring outside now. Can't this wait until tomorrow?" Sandy said.

"He's right, Becca," Rita said. "A couple cans of soup aren't worth getting soaked for. Besides, the house is locked up and my meager supplies aren't going anywhere."

OOO

In the pharmacy, Dr. Jones placed various medications into a cloth shopping bag after writing down what he was taking and putting the heavier drugs in the secure safe. Not knowing if Rita had gotten her prescription filled, he added insulin to the bag just in case, along with more bandages for Casey. From his office on the second floor, he retrieved his black bag, with his personal stethoscope, blood pressure monitor, and both digital and manual thermometers. He added a couple of prepackaged scalpels and a variety of sutures to be on the safe side, plus a few common medications.

"I think that's all I'll need," he said to the sheriff, and making sure the light switches were off, he locked the pharmacy doors. When the power was restored, he didn't want lights on to bring attention to the medical building. He collected his few overnight clothes from the physician's private sleeping quarters in the clinic and met Casey at the counter.

"I thought a little black bag was a relic from the past," Casey commented, snickering.

"We still use them for house calls. We just rarely make house calls anymore," he said with a shrug, and then they both left through the emergency room doors and locked those too.

At the sheriff's office, Casey collected some clothes, and then loaded up all the spare firearms into a jail cell along with the ammo, covered it all with a blanket, locked the cell, and pocketed all the keys. He had kept out two boxes of ammo that fit his personal sidearm, plus two 12-gauge shotguns and a box of shells.

"I would have thought the municipal buildings at the very least would have backup generators," Micah said, looking around at the darkened halls.

"Nope, never enough in the budget for that seldom-needed extravagance. We do have emergency lighting along the floors, but that's on a battery system and runs for only an hour or two so everyone can vacate the building. Those batteries would have been drained before we knew the power was out. I think the clinic has the same system," Casey explained, locking the doors as they left.

"I'm going to take a loop around town before going back to Becca's. Hope you don't mind the detour," Casey said.

"I don't mind. I'm just thankful I have a secure place to stay. Becca is really nice taking both of us in."

"She's a nice person, Doc, always has been," Casey said, keeping his eyes on the clusters of teenagers that seemed to be on nearly every corner.

"If you don't mind me saying so, you two seem to be ... friendly."

Casey laughed. "Friendly? We dated in high school and have stayed friends over the years. She got married, I didn't. She's now single again. Some feelings never die, Doc. And before you ask, I have been and will continue to sleep on the couch. And for the record, I'm going to do my damnedest to win her heart again and pity the man that tries to get in my way." He cut up the nearest side street when he saw the TV reporters look his way as they approached the cluster of teens. That TV crew seemed to be everywhere.

OOO

"What's this, Mom?" Meg asked, reading the note that was left on the table.

Sandy read the note over his sister's shoulder. "Wasn't this Lisa just here?"

Becca tried to grab the note from her daughter, but Rita got it first.

"You weren't meant to see that," Becca said to her children.

"Why not, Becca? They have a right to know what kind of a man their father is," Rita shouted. She turned to the two shocked teens. "This is who your father is, really is." She jabbed her finger at the note she returned to the table. "And two lives are now lost because of him—because he can't keep his pants zipped."

Sandy and Meg were shocked at Rita's bluntness, yet with the recent revelations about their father, they understood what she was getting at.

OOO

Justin set his paddle down on the long, green ping pong table and leaned forward on his hands with an audible sigh, eyes downcast. Sandy looked intently at him and laid his paddle down too.

"Yeah, I'm bored too," Sandy groaned, recognizing the look on his friend's face.

"If it weren't so hot, what would you be doing?"

Sandy looked around the brightly lit basement for a moment before answering. "Honestly, I'd probably hop on my bike and go to the beach."

"Think your mom would let us go?" Justin asked hopefully.

"I don't think we're under house arrest or anything, and we would be staying together." He paused. "That is, if you don't mind riding Meg's bike."

OOO

"Just be sure to *stay* together like the sheriff said, and take a bottle of water with you." Becca really didn't like the idea of the boys leaving the protection of the house, but from what Casey had told her privately, the killer had attacked only the vulnerable: the weak or old. Two strong, healthy boys should be safe. She also understood them needing to do something, *anything*, to relieve the boredom of being cooped up in the house all day.

OOO

With Kapac being *his* town, Sandy led the way, winding his route through the subdivision until the beach came in sight. The baseball cap he wore offered minimal shade to his face, and sunglasses shielded his eyes from the persistent glare. Sweat trickled down his back and into the waistband of his shorts.

"I forgot how free it feels to ride a bike!" Justin grinned. "And we kick up our own breeze. This feels great." Sweat began to bead on his forehead as soon as they stopped. He removed his cap and wiped his face with the back of his hand.

"The bonus to riding a bike is that it's almost 100 percent quiet," Sandy said, snickering.

"Are you thinking what I think you're thinking?"

"No one said we couldn't check out the barricades." Sandy straddled his bike for a long moment. "I heard Casey and my mom talking last night. Neither of them thinks there is any real danger anymore. What would it hurt to go look?" He pushed off before Justin could say a word of protest.

Sandy pedaled casually yet steadily toward the nearest blockade at the south end of town and slowed when the soldiers spotted them. One of the uniformed held up his hand to signal stop, and then pointed back the way the boys had come from. Justin waved and turned his bike around, Sandy following his movements.

Justin sighed. "Well, at least we know they are still here."

"Yeah, but if we could get to County Road 510, we would be on the other side of the blockade to see better, and I know how to get there!" Sandy announced. "My dad showed me a back way in from 510 that puts us on Luna Lake Road, right near the campground. That road is pretty overgrown, but I'm sure I can find it again."

Justin grinned widely. The thought of doing something so covert and possibly dangerous spiked his adrenalin and sent his heart racing.

"It's more overgrown than I remembered." Sandy scowled at the debris blocking their way. Small trees had fallen across the narrow road, blocking their progress, and shrubs were beginning to grow. "An SUV could probably drive over this without a problem but not our bikes."

"If it's not far, I say we leave the bikes here and walk it, just to scout it out, ya know? And walking would be even quieter." Justin was not about to give up yet.

They leaned the bikes against a large oak tree a few feet from the path and set out to cover the rest of the distance on foot, hopping over a larger downed tree shortly after.

"If it's okay with you," Justin whispered, "I'd like to take the lead and practice some of the stealth moves I've learned in ROTC."

With a bow and a grin, Sandy silently swept his arm, giving his permission for Justin to take over. They walked quietly along the path, avoiding deep piles of crunchy leaves and twigs that might snap under their weight. The spongy moss that normally grew in the wooded shade was dry, but the noise of the short growth was minimal.

A few minutes later, Justin paused and raised his right fist signaling Sandy to stop. He turned around and without words, motioned he had heard something. They crept slowly forward until they could see the dirt and gravel of 510 with several military tents pitched on the other side of the road. Another few slow feet and they could see more tents on their side of the road too. Crouching low to the ground, Justin used the silence of hand signals and led them away, back down the way they came.

Away from the tents, Justin admitted they were in over their heads and felt it could get dangerous if they were discovered.

As the two boys retrieved the bikes and sat straddling, they heard the roar of an engine coming from behind them. Now in panic mode, they pedaled as hard as they could and were soon at Luna Lake Road.

"This way!" Sandy called in a loud whisper and led Justin to the campground entrance where he veered to the left. At the now empty campground store, he jumped off his bike and leaned it against the building out of sight, tossed his hat to the ground and sprinted toward the lake.

Shorts and tank tops were the perfect swimwear, and they blended in with the rest of the campers. Justin dove underwater as soon as he was above knee deep.

"Sandy," he sputtered when he came up for air, "you're a genius!" and casually splashed water at Sandy when he saw a military jeep circling the campground. "Not to mention this feels great. I was really getting overheated."

They playfully splashed more water at each other as though they weren't aware they were being hunted by those in the jeep.

"Well, we didn't find out anything new, other than the military is camping out on 510," Justin said when they finally got out of the lake.

"But it was exciting." Sandy laughed, walking his bike down the hot beach toward town. "And I think it would be better if we didn't say anything to anyone about what we did. My mom might ground us for a month!"

CHAPTER FIFTEEN

Colter Iames sat at the cashier's counter in the Luna Landing minimart, watching the rain pounding down while keeping a wary eye on the small group of boys darting from shelter to shelter, heading in his direction. He picked up the shotgun from its resting place behind the counter, laid it across the glass top in full view, and picked up the book he had been reading.

The four boys, ranging in age from 13 to 17, were now huddled under the canopy that covered the silent gas pumps. Even though it was only 3:00 pm, the heavy clouds siphoned most of the light away, leaving just enough for the oldest to see Colter sitting inside.

"Mr. Colter, sir," the oldest said as the other three filed in behind him. "Is there anything left here to eat?" Many of the kids in town thought Colter was his last name. It didn't matter to him.

"There are some candy bars," Colter said flatly.

"I doubt if my mom would eat candy bars, but thank you anyway."

"You're looking for food for your mother?" Colter's interest was piqued. It was his experience that the kids these days were more concerned for themselves and had little interest in the welfare of their parents. This boy was familiar and his brain started shifting through memories to place him.

"Yes, sir, and water. I think I'll have to walk over to the campground to get that."

"You're Alex, right? I've seen you in here getting gas for that Camaro you drive."

Alex grinned. "Took me all summer last year to rebuild it, but she runs like a top now."

The more the boy talked, the more Colter remembered him: well-spoken, polite, and courteous. "There is some water over in the end cooler. It isn't cold, but it's wet. You boys help yourselves to two bottles each, and don't forget a couple for your mom."

When the boys returned to the counter, Colter handed Alex a fistful of granola bars.

"Now, the deal here is when you have finished the water, which is free, bring the empties back here so I can refill them and any others you can find. And those bars are for your mom, and these are for you boys," he said, handing out four large-sized candy bars.

"Thank you, sir," Alex said, his eyes dampening.

"I've also got a proposition for you, Alex—a job, if you want it."

"What kind of a job, Mr. Colter?"

"You bring that car of yours here and I'll put a couple gallons of gas in it every day so you can refill the water bottles for me at the campground. I've been giving away bottles of water to whoever asks or needs it, and I don't want to run out. Going to the campground is time-consuming for me and takes me away from minding the store here."

Alex's younger brother Joey finished his bottle and started to crush the plastic container. Alex smacked him on the back of the head. "Weren't you paying attention? He needs these bottles to refill, you nitwit!"

Colter smiled.

OOO

"Good afternoon from WROL here in sunny Dresden, and I'm Cynthia Thompson."

"And I'm meteorologist Don Drake. At the top of our stories today is the strange weather happening in Kapac. While everyone else is enjoying moderate temperatures in the 80s, Kapac is now well over 100 for the fourth day in a row with heavy rain. This weather just seems to hang on top of that town smothering it in oppressive humidity like someone has tethered it there."

"Oh, come on, Don, you can't be saying there is something going on that is influencing the weather."

"Well, if you look at this map ..." he started to say.

"We all know that weather modification is pure fiction—a conspiracy theory that no one with a half a brain really believes in," Cynthia said with smirk. "And now for the sports," she continued, completely cutting him off from mentioning anything more about the strange weather in Kapac.

OOO

John Tasen finished his can of cold soup, rinsed it out in the waste basket they had filled with water from the lake, and put it in the trash bag that was getting full and starting to smell. They needed to find a dumpster soon.

"I'm getting tired of cold food," he moaned.

"We should have gotten some candles at that store. I could have rigged something to heat a can," Harry said. "At least we have food to eat though."

"That's true, and thanks to you. Come on, Harry, let's go walk the beach and talk to people."

"That's gotta be better than sitting around all day." Harry picked up his camera. "Uh, John, the battery is almost dead.

Do we have enough gas in the van to drive for a while to recharge?"

"Well, there's enough to get over to that gas station. Let's do that first, and then see if we can find the sheriff before he sneaks away again."

CHAPTER SIXTEEN

August 13
Sunday

"I think we should get the rest of my food over here before it starts raining again," Rita said, looking at the puddles shimmering in the driveway.

"I'll go with you," Casey offered. "Justin, will you come with us, please? I can't carry as much as I would normally. Becca, do you have any extra cloth bags?"

She handed Justin the bags. "I know it's only across the street, but take my car and pull into the garage to unload. We don't want anyone accidentally seeing what you've got." She scowled. Becca had always been generous and the thought of being selfish and keeping things from her neighbors didn't sit well with her.

Rita opened her front door, frowning, certain she had locked it, but said nothing. In the kitchen, she opened cupboard after cupboard and said, "Not as much as I thought was here, but take it all. I'm going after a few things in my office." She left them before Casey could stop her. Even though it had been only a few days, Rita was feeling overwhelmed being around so many people all the time. She was too accustomed to her solitary life.

"Casey!" she called out a few moments later.

He rushed toward the voice, recognizing the sound of fear. Rita stood in the open doorway to her private office. Casey saw the cause of her concern: the office had been trashed. He stepped around her with his gun drawn, looking behind the door, in the closet, and behind the couch. The room wasn't very big and had very few places for someone to hide. The room was currently clear of any unwanted guests.

"I gather you didn't leave the room like this," he said. The desktop computer had been smashed, the monitor was shattered, and a pile of thumb drives had been pulverized with a hammer that was still there on the floor. Nothing else had been touched. "Someone wanted to send you a message, Rita. Remind me what it is you do?"

"I'm a computer systems analyst, and I design websites on the side," she whispered. The destruction was concise and deliberate, and it had nothing to do with that job. She was sure it was her covert work that was at the heart of this. And that scared her because not one of *those* clients knew who or where she really was, or so she thought.

"Hopefully, your house insurance will cover the damage," Casey said. "You got a camera to take pictures? I'll file an official report for you."

Rita almost declined, and then she thought it might look less suspicious if she did make a claim, and pulled out her phone and started snapping pictures.

"Is this your hammer?"

"No," she answered. When she took a closer look at it, chills went down her spine: It was exactly like the one she found in her car, a replica of her new 'calling card' that she left behind when she broke into a system: a Thor-like mallet. "Let's get out of here." She tried staying calm, tamping down the fear growing in the pit of her stomach.

OOO

"This will help out a great deal, Rita, thanks," Becca said, putting the soup cans with her own and lining up the boxed cereals and easy-to-fix mixes on the counter. "You seem on edge—are you feeling okay?"

"Someone broke into my house and trashed my office," Rita admitted. "Completely destroying my desktop system."

"All of your work gone?"

Rita took Becca's hand and walked her out onto the deck. The air was still humid and heavy, but the deck gave them the privacy Rita needed for her confession.

"I can't go into everything I do, Becca, but I can tell you, and only you, that the office set-up is a dummy ... or was. Oh, it really worked, and it held my personal email, games, certain innocuous search engines, and the such, but my laptop upstairs is my real work. It's very private and very ... dangerous if it falls into the wrong hands."

"Are we here in danger, Rita?"

"I don't know."

OOO

"Mom!" Meg called out. "Did you forget to pay the internet bill? I can't get any service."

"That's the first bill I pay, Meg." Becca grinned at her daughter. "Is your phone working?"

"That's working, but it won't connect to the internet. Yesterday, I could read mail but not send ... now I can't even read anything." Meg punched a few numbers and Becca's phone rang. "See? I tried calling my friend Sara, and I go right to voicemail. Maybe her phone isn't charged like ours are."

With everyone suddenly without internet, even those on different servers, Rita disappeared upstairs. Becca followed her and watched as Rita booted up her laptop and logged on.

"So why do you have internet and we don't?" Becca asked quietly after closing the door.

Rita pursed her lips. "Because I hook onto a satellite, a government satellite. I *always* have access. I also have a phone that connects to a government server."

"Rita Martin, are you telling me you're a spy?" Becca half-joked, placing her fists on her narrow hips.

Rita laughed. "No, I'm not a spy. I'm not a secret agent or anything like that. Please, Becca, don't ask me anything. I really can't tell you! And don't let the kids know I have internet."

"When Casey and Micah come back, you have to tell Casey what you can. If all our communications are suddenly down, something is more wrong than some elusive toxic spill." Becca paced thoughtfully and then faced Rita. "Shut down. Something is definitely not adding up."

Becca turned on the TV in the living room, and a blue screen flashed then cleared. The national weather station was playing like it always did on a Sunday afternoon. She started flipping channels and stopped when WROL in Dresden came on. She unmuted the TV and watched.

"... WROL in Dresden." Cynthia Thompson turned to face a different camera. "Unfortunately, Kapac Days has been cancelled by the city officials due to the extreme heat. Temperatures running 105 degrees and above is considered to be too much of a health risk. Perhaps they will reschedule for next weekend. There have also been some delays with the CDC fogging, but it will commence when the rain stops so stay close to your shelter." Cynthia smiled at the weatherman. "Well, Don, the warm weather got a bit too warm this time it would seem."

"So it does. Has there been any further word on the power failure in Kapac?" the weather man asked, eliciting a thin-lipped scowl from Cynthia.

"Only that they're working on it and will keep us informed when they have further information," she answered coldly. "Any further word on the weather?" she asked sarcastically.

"Yes, Cynthia, this high-pressure system seems to still be stuck. However, there is another front coming down from Canada that should relieve some of this humidity," Don Drake said, ignoring Cynthia's tone. "Elsewhere in the country, we are seeing heavy rains from Tropical Storm Irving." Becca muted the TV again.

"Why didn't they give us an update on the toxic spill?" Sandy asked. "And if the city officials aren't even here like Casey said, how is it they sound like they know what's going on?"

"Have any of you seen the fogging that was to be done? Or any CDC trucks driving around?" Becca asked. "This is just too weird," she said when no one had. "Okay, so we have TV and phones because we have power, though no one else does. And they keep saying we'll be fogged but it doesn't happen. It sounds like they just want to keep us indoors while they keep crying wolf at us."

OOO

When Rita silently went up the stairs to her room, Becca followed.

"You have that determined look on your face. Something is definitely on your mind."

"I had an idea. Give me a few minutes, okay?" Rita said, powering up her computer again. Becca sat down on the twin bed across from her and waited.

"What are you doing?" Becca asked after a few minutes, amazed at the speed Rita's fingers flew across the keyboard.

"Shh! I need to concentrate." Rita stared at the screen, typed, scrolled, stop to read something, typed again. She opened multiple windows and closed a few. After ten minutes, she turned to Becca, her face passive yet angry. "I'm in the private files of the CDC. Come and look at this document."

"You hacked into the CDC? Rita!"

"Keep your voice down! Don't worry, no one can trace me. Besides, although this information is not meant for the public, it isn't classified either. Now look!"

The page was titled simply "investigations."

"So, what am I looking at exactly?"

"This is a list of all the CDC investigations for the last six months, both open cases and closed ones, arranged by date. Closed cases have this mark next to them." Rita pointed to a "C" at the end of the identifying location. "Anything jump out at you?"

Becca read for a bit and then went back to the beginning. "This one in Alabama is from yesterday. Where's Kapac?"

"Give that gal a kewpie doll." Rita's voice was low and on the edge of angry. "The CDC isn't here, never was. We don't have a harmful toxic spill in our town."

"Then why is the military keeping us locked down?"

"I don't know. Unless ..." Rita continued, half-talking to herself, "it isn't on this list, because it *is* classified." And to herself she added, *and even I can't get into that now because I already fixed the hole for them a few months ago.*

"We need to tell Casey what you found out, Rita."

"No, we don't! If word got out we were on to them, things could get a lot worse."

"Them who?"

"I don't know that either. The military? The government? Tipping our hand could put us all in danger, Becca." Rita shut down and closed her laptop, believing she was already in danger. "Promise me you won't say anything to anyone."

Becca frowned but agreed with a nod, willing to do anything to keep her family safe.

OOO

Once word got out and circulated through town that there was still water available, cars lined up in increasing numbers leading into the campground on the north side of Luna Lake. The line of people holding empty jugs waiting their turn at the hand pump was long and mostly quiet and respectful. The line moved steadily as one man continuously pumped the handle. He had two filled containers sitting at his feet and occasionally slipped a tin cup under the running water for a quick drink while working in the hot sun.

"Hey, get your cup out of there! It's my turn! Now pump!" a very elderly man screeched, holding out an empty milk jug with shaky hands.

"I'm only getting a sip of water so I can continue," the young man protested.

"Well, you can just wait. Pump, I said!"

"No," the young man said, letting go of the handle and the water slowed to a dribble. "I don't have to anymore. I've been pumping for everyone for almost an hour in this heat. I'm hot, tired, and my shoulder hurts. All I wanted was a drink. For that," the young man picked up his two jugs, "you can pump your own damn water now! I'm done!"

The old man stared at the retreating back. He looked at the next person in line. "You pump the water," he demanded.

"You just ruined a generous act for the rest of us. I think *you* should take a turn pumping water."

"But ... I've got arthritis in both shoulders, I can't ..." he whined.

"Well, pump yours and leave or get out of our way!" someone else called out from the long line. The old man picked up the handle and pumped, wincing at the pain. The water splashed down with only half of it going into the container he set under the spout.

The crowd started yelling and pushing with impatience. The old man picked up his half-filled water jug and backed away. He slipped on the wet grass and went down, spilling his water.

When he got up to refill the now empty jug, the next in line pushed him aside saying, "You've had your turn. Get to the end of the line."

As the old man stumbled to the end of the line, he heard someone say, "Isn't it amazing and pathetic how one selfish person can ruin a good thing."

CHAPTER SEVENTEEN

Casey drove slowly through the town after his twice-daily trip out to the barricades where they told him the same thing: nothing.

Leaves hung limp on the usually lush trees, the intense heat curling the edges. Any other time, he would have dispersed the groups of teens he found everywhere. Without backup, there was little he could do, and although Micah had volunteered to keep him company, Casey couldn't ask him to do anything else.

"Look over there!" Micah pointed to the strip of businesses on the opposite side of Highway 21. Casey slowed and watched several boys breaking the windows of the electronics and appliance store. From a safe distance, they watched as the kids carried out big flat-screen TVs and computers, looting whatever they could carry and run with.

"What has gotten into them? They can't even use those without power and this is such a small town, these things will be very easy to find." Casey groaned in helplessness as he pulled a notepad from the glove box and jotted down the date and a few names. "That redhead there, would you believe that's the minister's son? These kids have gone crazy." The next three that came out of the store had small tablets and were jabbing their fingers at them frantically. When the devices didn't function as they expected, the boys threw the small computers on the sidewalk and stomped on them in frustration before running off.

"There is a clinical term for this, Sheriff: it's called mass mentality or mass hysteria. People, especially vulnerable ones like kids, are easily goaded or convinced into doing things they normally wouldn't think of doing during times of intense stress. Like the minister's son," Dr. Micah said calmly. "I remember talking to a camp counselor back when I was an intern. Some of the young girls in her group were stable, outdoorsy girls; but when there were wasps in the main cabin, and a few of the other girls got scared and started crying, even the girls who weren't afraid at all got caught up in the hysteria and fell apart. What are you going to do here?"

"There's not a damn thing I can do," Casey said. "On the other hand, I can sure as hell try to find out how long this will last!" He turned the squad car around and headed out to the roadblock yet again.

OOO

Casey drove right up to the barricade and got out of the car. He stomped over to the nearest soldier who stayed a good ten feet behind the barrier and got as in his face as possible.

"What the hell is going on here?" Casey shouted. Even though he had been there earlier, this soldier was new, another unfamiliar face.

"Please, sir, get back in your vehicle and return home."

"Vehicle? You see that? It's the sheriff's squad car and I'm the sheriff! Now I want some answers!"

"There's been a toxic spill and the town is still under quarantine."

"Yeah, I know all about the spill. I was one of the first ones on the scene," Casey said looking around. "And just where is the white van that was on its side, with the cargo of open canisters spilling out the back? If it's not still here, then the site has been cleaned up. And if it's cleaned up, I want these barricades down and I want my deputies allowed back into my town—NOW!" Casey describing the spill had unnerved the man.

The young soldier kept his face stony, but Casey could see the fear and doubt in his eyes as he backed away. "I'll get my CO for you to talk to, Sheriff, sir." And the young man hurried away, stopping at the back of a troop carrier. Casey could hear the soft whirr of a small air conditioner, and he surmised it was installed on the opposite side of the canvas covering so no one from town could see it.

The military officer stepped around the blockade of vehicles and came to within a few feet of the wooden barrier to face the sheriff.

Casey looked at the younger man who was still older than the guard and recognized the bars of rank. "What can you tell me that will make me happy, Lieutenant?"

He raised his eyebrows at the recognition. "How long were you in the service, Sheriff?"

"Ten years, and that's long enough to know when I'm being stonewalled."

"I'm Lt. Elias Murphy, sir. Your assumption is partly correct, except you're not being stonewalled without good reason. We are waiting for the final paperwork from the CDC to release the town from lockdown," Murphy said.

"Paperwork? That's it? It better be soon because my town is falling apart!" Casey sneered.

"Please come back here at noon tomorrow and I should be able to give you more information and a firm release time," Murphy said. He turned and went back to his office inside the converted troop carrier.

OOO

3:00 pm

"Going on rounds with you has been interesting, Casey," Dr. Micah said. "I didn't realize how boring it could get though." He chuckled.

"Do you want to go back to the clinic?" Casey asked cautiously.

"No, I hear Becca is making spaghetti tonight."

Casey laughed. "Yeah, she has turned into a really good cook. Seriously, though, if there is too much of a *crowd* there for you ..." Casey paused and slowed the car down to stop next to a young boy who was pacing with a phone in his hand. "Hey there, Tommy, is anything wrong?"

The boy looked up suddenly, realizing someone spoke to him. His eyes quickly went back to his phone. "It won't work," he said without looking up again.

Casey and Micah got out of the scout car and approached the boy.

"Can I see it?" Casey asked, holding out his big hand. Tommy stared at him with glazed eyes and handed the phone over. Casey immediately saw the cracks in the face of the delicate device. "Maybe the problem is that it's cracked, Tommy."

Tommy grabbed it back from the sheriff. "No! You don't understand, it won't work. It won't work. It won't work. It won't work. It won't work. It won't work. It won't work." His voice got louder and more agitated with each repetition. "It won't work!" The boy screeched and resumed his pacing.

"Maybe I should take you home. Your mom might let you use hers," Casey suggested, concerned with the level of anger pouring out of the boy.

"No! Hers doesn't work either. She tried to fix mine and that's how mine broke! She dropped it! The stupid bitch dropped my phone!" Tommy screamed.

Micah touched Casey's arm and motioned with his head to move away from the boy.

"Is that Thomas Bates?"

"Yeah, is he a patient of yours?"

"No, but his mother is. She was in the ER two weeks ago for cuts and bruises on her arms. She said she fell. Forensics is not my specialty, but I recognize defensive injuries when I see them," Micah explained. "Do you know the family?"

"I know most everyone in town, Doc, some better than others. I don't know the Bates really well, but I do know the father, Robert, was killed in a car accident almost a year ago. Tommy was in the car with him and the car was found in a ditch on 510—it wasn't spotted for almost twenty-four hours. Once he was extracted, he was catatonic for two weeks."

"Okay, makes more sense now. That boy is approaching if not already into a psychotic break." Micah's face contorted with pain. "We need to check on the mother."

Casey nodded.

"Hey, Tommy, let's go for a ride. It's nice and cool in my car," Casey suggested.

The boy's eyes shot up to the sheriff. "Yeah, okay, it's really hot out here." He climbed into the back seat where he couldn't get out and continued to punch the cellphone that wouldn't work.

A few blocks from the main drag in town, Casey turned onto Spring Street and stopped a few houses down.

"Is this your house, Tommy?"

The boy looked up, pivoting his head toward the green and white gingerbread house and stared blankly. "Yeah." He went back to watching the empty screen on the phone.

"You stay here where it's cool. We'll be right back," Casey instructed.

Micah raised his fist to knock and then noticed the door was already open.

"I don't like the looks of this," Casey muttered. "Mrs. Bates? Are you home? It's Sheriff WhiteCloud." They stepped inside. "Mrs. Bates?" he called again. "There's been a struggle—lamp broken, table overturned, and that looks like blood on the floor," he said to Micah, looking at the destruction in the living room.

"We need to find her."

In the kitchen, Tommy's mother was slumped over the table, head resting on her arms.

"Shit," Casey groaned. "This kid can't be our serial killer."

Micah pushed the dirty blonde hair away from her face to expose a nasty bruise and lifted her head. She moaned, startling the doctor.

"There aren't any other obvious injuries, Casey, other than that she's drunk."

"I'm going to bring Tommy in here."

"Can you bring a bottle of water back with you? I'll clean the head wound," Micah said.

"Hey, Tommy, come on inside. I've got a couple of questions for you." Casey opened the back door after grabbing a bottle of water from the front seat of the squad car.

"When was the last time you saw your mother, Tommy?" Casey asked when they stepped inside.

Tommy looked around the living room. "Maybe two or three hours ago. After she broke my phone, I pushed her away and she fell. Lazy bitch was taking a nap on the floor when I left."

"When she fell, she hit her head pretty hard, Tommy, and you just left her there on the floor?"

The boy snarled. "Yeah, I told you she broke my phone! I was really mad at her." Casey ushered him into the kitchen where Micah began washing the wound. Tommy looked at her and flatly said, "I'm going to my room." He stalked out and a few moments later, they heard a door slam.

"Is that kind of coldness typical of a break?" Casey asked the doctor.

"They are all different, though it isn't unusual." A gun fired in another part of the house, the echo bouncing off the walls.

Casey bolted down the hallway and stopped in front of three closed doors. The first one was the bathroom, and the odors coming from there had him closing the door before it was fully open. The second was a typical boy's room and empty. The final door was the master bedroom, and Tommy lay sprawled on the double bed, gun still in his hand and half of his head missing.

OOO

"He was only 14, Doc, why would he commit suicide like that?"

"Tommy was a very angry boy, and not just because his phone wouldn't work. It appears he completely lost his sense of reality. That kind of anger often gets turned inward. And I think it might be prudent to keep an eye out for more violent behavior from the youngsters."

"More? Smashing windows and looting isn't violent enough from otherwise nice kids?"

"Excellent point."

They had delivered Mrs. Bates to a neighbor, who promised to take care of her, and then covered Tommy with a yellow, flowered sheet, closed the door tightly as they had been doing for all the others, and went to find the mortician.

OOO

"These deaths are highly unusual, Sheriff," Joseph Johnson said, zipping up the body bag that held Tommy Bates.

"They sure are, Mr. Johnson. Suicides and murders are not normal for our quiet town." Casey stood aside while the mortician and his son lifted the child onto a gurney and wheeled it out to the hearse. "And with all that's happening, we would be in an even bigger mess if you weren't on a generator to keep the, um, freezers going."

"Let's hope the power comes back on soon, Sheriff, or I might have to start charging you rent!" the elderly man joked. Getting serious, he added, "Even though I recently got my yearly shipment of Tyvek body bags, remember, Sheriff, there are only six freezers in the morgue. There's only room for one more, and I would hate to have to stack them."

"With as friendly as the town is, can I ask why you call him *Mr.* Johnson, and not Joe or Joseph?" Micah asked after the two had left with their gruesome cargo.

Casey thought for a moment about the question. "Perhaps it's a sign of respect for someone with a job no one else wants. And perhaps we don't want to get too close to him for the same reason."

CHAPTER EIGHTEEN

5:00 pm

Mostly to avoid the WROL news van parked in front of his office, Casey cruised down Kapac Boulevard, the second and original business district in town. Locals knew of the shops of course, but many tourists did not. The main business area, with its restaurants, ice cream parlors, T-shirt shops, and gifts stores, were all the visitors were interested in—not the hardware store or appliance shop. The Boulevard, as the locals called it, was mostly deserted. The businesses, usually bustling with activity, stood vacant and silent. The exception was a few people lingering under the limited shade of the many trees. Even at the late hour, the sun beat down unmercifully.

Casey slowed when he got to Mins Butcher Shoppe, where Jessica Nelson had stocked up on some limited foods for the church retreat. From under the large shade tree out front, the broken windows were easy to spot from the road.

"Stay with the car, okay, Micah? I need to check this out," Casey said, leaving the patrol car running. He eased the front door open across the shattered glass and stepped inside. The shelves and display tables were knocked over and stripped clean of anything edible; the meat cases were bare. With the cases still closed and intact, it was as if they were emptied orderly. That's when he noticed the padlocked coolers down the short hall behind the counter. After checking and finding the padlocks secure, he pulled out his phone and called John Mins' landline.

"John, this is Sheriff WhiteCloud—your shop has been broken into. Can you meet me here? And it might be better if you come to the back door."

"Everything okay?" Micah asked.

"I don't know yet," Casey said. Getting back into his car, he drove around the block and parked behind the butcher store to wait for the owner. He pulled out his checkbook from the glove compartment, checked his balance, then made out a check. A few minutes later, John stopped behind him.

"The front was broken into, John, and the place is cleaned out," Casey told him. "I did notice you have padlocks on the coolers and they're intact. Do you have food in there?"

John sighed. "Yeah. After I found out about the lockdown, I took some of the perishables home and put the rest in the store freezer—a freezer that now doesn't have any power."

"Even with it warm, if those doors haven't been opened, the food could well be fine, if not still frozen," Micah added. "But it won't stay that way for long."

"Why don't we have a look, John? If the food is okay, I have an offer for you," Casey said, following John into the back room of the silent store, where the owner pulled out a set of keys and removed the padlocks.

"This is the freezer." He opened the door only enough to feel the cool air rushing out then closed it again. "Sheriff, we just might have caught a break. Let's look in the cooler where the baked goods and cheeses are." The air was stale but still cooler than the room was. John reached for the light switch and then laughed. "Sorry. Habit."

Casey produced a flashlight and they stepped inside. Shelves held a supply of multiple varieties of cheese and packages of bread and buns. John reached out and ran his hand along the cheese packaging.

"Still cool, but not cold as it should be. Can I see your flashlight for a minute, Sheriff?" John looked at the refrigerator's thermostat. "Sixty-five degrees. This will need to be used quickly, but most of it should still be good." He looked at Casey. "If the freezer is below fifty degrees, the meat is good and yeah, some might even still be frozen." He nodded toward the doctor, acknowledging his earlier assessment.

"There doesn't seem to be all that much in the cooler," Micah commented.

"That's because I put everything else in the freezer: beef, pork, sausage, chicken, and all the lunchmeats," John explained, "after I took a lot of it home." John's thoughts flashed back to his time during the Detroit riots and how the neighbors ransacked his shop, leaving him and his family nothing.

They closed the cooler door and stepped into the freezer where the air felt much colder than the cheese room. Casey flashed his light around until he found the thermostat on the wall.

"It says fifty-two degrees," Casey said, reading the battery-operated digital device.

"Close enough!" John grinned in the dark. "What's your offer, Sheriff? How much of this do you want?" Now he understood what the sheriff was preparing to bargain for and why he had him come to the back door.

Casey handed him the check he had already written out. "This much. Whatever you feel is fair, John."

John raised his eyebrows. "May I ask where this is going?"

"You know Becca Burns, right? She's taken in kids from the church camp and neighbors, eight altogether now, and she's running low on food," Casey said, side-stepping the small details, such as he was one of those that was taken in.

"Becca is a good person."

"She sure is. She would probably take in more if she had the room." Casey laughed.

"Since this is mine, I'll take some for myself and my family, and a couple of boxes with me to drop off at the church camp. You can take the rest and we'll call it even."

They collected empty boxes and Styrofoam totes from the store stockroom and loaded everything they could. John was taking more lunch meats and burger to the camp; roasts, steaks and some chicken went into his van; and a mixed supply of everything else went into the squad car trunk and back seat.

"I feel more optimistic right now than I've felt in a week," Micah said. "Can I ask how much that check was for?"

"No, you can't. Let's just say it was a lot, and worth every penny. Come on, we need to get this back into Becca's freezer and fridge."

OOO

Tyler Wanes and his three buddies were strolling down the near-empty Boulevard at the same time Casey had pulled around the back of the butcher shop. Hidden by the shade of the trees, they followed the scout car going in the same direction so they could stay behind the sheriff unseen. Watching the activity from behind a dumpster, Ty saw an opportunity and hatched a plan.

Ty sneered. "There was still food in that place we didn't find. Now that the sheriff has it, we can get to it. All we have to do is find out where he parks at night. Let's take a walk around town." He idly wondered where Doug had gone; he hadn't been part of the gang since they broke into the donut shop.

OOO

John Mins drove up to the church retreat's locked gate that fronted on the loop road going around Luna Lake and rang the buzzer, one of the few things that had been updated to wireless and ran on batteries.

Jessica peered out a window then went down to open the gate. She hesitated and asked, "What do you want, John? Casey said we shouldn't open the gates to anyone."

"I understand, Jess, but Casey and I just emptied the freezer at the shop. Things are thawing and I thought you could use some extra food for the kids," he explained.

Her eyes lit up and she opened the lock. John drove in and up the short distance to the main house where the kitchen was. By the time she walked back, he was almost done unloading the boxes he had set aside for the camp.

"Bless you, John!" She wept once she saw what he was giving her.

"Just keep those children—and yourself—safe, Jess." He got back in his van and waited for her to unlock and relock the security gate, making sure all was secure before he left.

OOO

Casey drove the scout car up Becca's drive, stopped and turned around, backing up to the garage. He and Micah went to the front door and knocked so they could be seen from inside.

Becca smiled when she saw the two and opened the door.

Casey grinned. "We have a surprise. Open the garage door." They went back to the car and started unloading box after box. Once everything was in the garage, Casey lowered the door, leaving his scout car parked on the concrete drive next to Becca's, and went inside.

"What are you being so secretive about?" Becca gave him a playful smile.

He cupped her face with his big hands and gave her a deep kiss. "Our luck just changed," he said. "Ask the kids to come up and give us a hand."

With all the boxes and coolers lined up on the kitchen floor, Casey started opening them, exposing a box of three beef roasts, one with burger, another of six chickens, yet another of cheese, until he had opened up eight boxes of various sizes.

Becca was stunned. "Where ... no, don't tell me. I really don't want to know."

Casey laughed. "It's okay, Becca. I paid John Mins for all of this."

It took them almost a half hour to re-sort all the foods: some going into the near-empty refrigerator, some into the freezer side, and the rest into the deep freeze in the basement.

Becca was on the verge of tears. "Unless this lockdown lasts for another month, we will be fine now." She gave Casey a long hug.

After they treated themselves to a feast of hotdogs that were one of the first things to start thawing once removed from the butcher's freezer, they all sat in the living room, watching a movie like one big extended family until someone knocked on the front door.

Meg was closest and looked out the small window and reached for the doorknob.

"Don't open the door!" Becca said a fraction of a second too late.

"It's okay, Mom, I recognize him from school." As soon as the lock was disengaged, the boy shouldered the door open, knocking Meg down. The four boys rushed in with Ty in the lead holding a gun.

"Oooh, man, does it feel good in here! You've got to be the only one in town with electricity to run the a/c. I think we're going to like it here!" Ty said with a demented grin, waving the gun around. "And I smell food! Get us some, now!"

"Put the gun down, Tyler," Casey said, standing.

"Ya know, Sheriff, maybe I should just finish what I started a few days ago and shoot you. At this range, I won't miss again," Ty said, taking a step toward Casey.

Tawny stepped forward, blocking his way. "You're cute. You wouldn't shoot *me*, would you?" she said sweetly, flirting with the unbathed and grungy-looking young man.

"Oh, baby." He looked at her from head to toe. "No, I wouldn't. I think I've got plans for you."

Sandy moved forward, but Justin stopped him. "Wait," he whispered.

Tawny smiled seductively and moved closer, bringing her hands up as if to caress him. In a lightning fast move, she knocked the gun out of his hand, breaking his wrist, then throat punched him and kicked the gun aside. His eyes rolled back in his head as he collapsed without a sound. One of the other boys grabbed her from behind and without hesitation, she held onto the arms that encircled her, took a step forward and leaned down, which threw him off balance. With the momentum, she then stepped backward, sending him over her head. Still holding onto one of his arms, she pulled it up and kicked him in the armpit, dislocating his shoulder. As the last two rushed her, she quickly spun gracefully and delivered a roundhouse kick to the head of the nearest one, knocking him out cold. Turning to the last one, she side-kicked him in the groin. He staggered back a foot, curled into a fetal position, and folded like a deflated balloon. It all took less than 30 seconds.

Sandy stared and Justin laughed. "Good going, little sister!" Justin turned to Sandy. "She's been taking ballet since she was five and karate since she was ten. She's ready for her black belt, but doesn't want to test until she's 18."

"That was so ... Summer Glau! You're amazing, Tawny!" Sandy said, still stunned and in awe of what he had just witnessed.

Tawny grinned. "You think so? Thanks! She's my idol."

Justin helped Meg off the floor and continued to hold her hand as he put his other arm around her shoulders.

Casey was as stunned as everyone else. "Maybe I should deputize you, Tawny!" He turned toward Becca's son and tossed the keys to his scout car. "Sandy, there are zip tie handcuffs in my glove box. Would you get them, please?"

Micah hovered over the inert teens. He felt the shoulder on one, and kneeling on the boy's chest, put his shoulder back in place with a firm yank. Assessing the other two, he said, "This one will have one hell of a headache and this one might pee blood for a day or two." He knelt beside Ty, felt his wrist, then his throat. "Casey, come here."

In whispers, Micah said, "This one is dead. His hyoid bone is intact and the larynx doesn't feel crushed, yet it's is so swollen it appears to have blocked off the trachea and he couldn't breathe. I'm sure she pulled the punch, so I'm guessing he had some previous damage or an underlying condition, which wouldn't surprise me."

OOO

Becca turned to her daughter. "Meg, this is exactly why Casey said not to open the door to anyone. Even though you recognized one of them from school, it didn't mean you could trust him. There are several levels of knowing a person. You knew that boy for a year or so from school, but you didn't really know him well enough to trust him. And you've known Justin for a week or two, yet you know him to be the kind of person you can trust.

"I've known your father for eighteen years, yet now I realize I don't really know him at all, and I certainly can't trust him." Becca looked at Meg's embarrassment. "Do you understand the difference?"

"Yes, Mom, and I'm really sorry. It won't happen again."

OOO

After the boys were removed to the jail and Tyler to the morgue, a very tired sheriff and doctor went back to what was now home for them, for some much-needed sleep—Micah to the basement and Casey to the couch.

Becca quietly slipped out of her room and sought the peace of the back deck to sort out her thoughts. *What a difference in my life a few days have made,* she thought. So much was happening and it was overloading her senses. She breathed in the humid air that hung in the night, only the lack of sunshine making it cooler than the day. It was oppressing and depressing to not see the stars, and the woods seemed ominous and threatening for the first time in her life. She shivered.

Quiet as she was, Casey had become sensitive to her presence. He could feel her energy whenever she walked into or out of a room. He came up behind her and said, "You should wear your hair down more often—it makes finding your neck more fun." He brushed her hair aside and kissed her shoulder. "Are you okay?" he asked when she didn't immediately respond.

She silently shook her head and leaned into him. "No, Casey, I'm not okay. I'm just not used to this kind of violence. I don't think I could ever be." She sighed, leaning further into him. "I'm scared. I'm scared for these children. I'm scared for what the town has become."

He put his arms around her from behind. "I won't let anything or anyone hurt you or the kids. I promise."

Becca turned inside the circle of his arms to face him. "Promise?"

"On my life."

She pulled his face to hers and kissed him deeply.

"How's your arm feel?" she asked with a knowing smile then reached up and ran her fingers through his shortened hair.

"What arm?" He grinned in the dark. "Are you sure, Becca?" he asked gently, his voice a bare whisper in the dark.

"Yes, I am. You were my first love, Casey, and I still love you. I think I always have."

She wrapped her arms around his neck and kissed him again. He pulled her in tight and deepened the kiss. Becca sank into his body instantly, the hard contours of his body enfolding her. She took a step away and took him by the hand, silently leading him to her bedroom.

CHAPTER NINETEEN

Two dozen men and women sat around a blazing fire at the dark campground. The fire was for light, not for heat, and one by one they pushed their rickety lawn chairs back away from the hot flames.

"It's great having all the water we want, but I'm still hungry, and water doesn't help that."

"Yeah, and my kids ate the last of the cereal I had hidden," one thirty-ish woman said.

"When it gets light enough to see, I'm going back to that grocery store and find out if there's anything left," Adam Raines said.

"But we can't get to Walstroms," another commented.

"I'm not talking about Walstroms. There's a small grocery on the other side of the park here in town. I was there the day before the power went out and he still had lots of food, just not much fresh stuff. Who wants to go with me?"

"I didn't know about that store."

"Not many do. His prices are a lot higher than Walstroms."

From the outer edge, hidden within the shadows, a deep voice with a southern accent called out, "Why wait until tomorrow? Let's go now! We can light the place up with our headlights and I don't care about the prices. We can just take what we need!"

Six cars and three pickup trucks left the grounds, following the one who said he knew where the store was.

OOO

Adam turned his big truck around in the parking lot of Lindens Grocery and put his high beams on, illuminating the large glass door. The others did the same, lining up and aiming their headlights at the shade-drawn windows.

Adam jumped into the back of his truck, and with a self-satisfied smirk, produced a long-handled axe. Striding up to the door, he swung it, cracking the glass. Another two forceful swings and the glass shattered, and everyone rushed in, stepping carelessly over the sharp shards.

One woman stumbled around in the darkness for a few minutes, then went to the large windows and opened the shades, flooding the store with light from all the parked vehicles. She grabbed a shopping cart and the first thing she took were four boxes of disposable diapers, then juice bottles, cookies, potato chips, and cans of beans. In a frenzy now, she grabbed anything she could get her hands on and tossed it into her basket, whether she needed it or not.

It was a madhouse with everyone pushing and shoving to get at what they wanted or what they could reach. Others from the campground had followed and added to the chaos. Stale cereal littered the floor when there was a fight over the last box of some sugary treat and the fragile cardboard split. One by one, each person pushed a cart out to their car and emptied it all into their back seat ... and left.

OOO

Carl Linden saw the vehicles pulling in from his overhead view of his parking lot. Alarmed, he stood very still and just watched. He flinched when he heard the glass door shatter, but he stayed rooted where he was. He was swamped with harsh and painful memories of the riots he lived through in Detroit.

The yelling and screaming from below frightened him. Sounds of shelving toppling over seeped up from under his feet, yet he still didn't move for fear of alerting those ransacking his store to his presence.

Standing next to the window that had the bird's eye view of all the vehicles, Carl watched them leave, one by one until there was silence. The sheriff's office was on the other side of the park, but without phone service, he couldn't call for help. He wasn't sure the sheriff could do anything; he would come, but the elderly man had seen Casey with his arm in a sling and knew he was injured. Like others in the town, Carl was on his own.

Carl sat heavily on his couch, his head cradled in his liver-spotted hands, and wept.

CHAPTER TWENTY

August 14
Monday

"Okay, boys. I'm hoping that a night in jail has gotten the message across. I'm going to let you out. Go back to the campground, get your shit together, and stay out of trouble." Casey took the keys to the jail cell and unlocked it.

"Where's Tyler, sir?"

"Tyler is dead."

"He's dead? She killed him?" the boy asked in a whisper, still clutching his shoulder. They all stared at Casey. The scared look in their eyes said everything.

"No, he killed himself by being stupid. He picked the wrong person to mess with. Remember that."

"Yes, sir, but Tyler drove and he still has the keys to the car. We can't leave even if there wasn't a roadblock," Ken said, cradling his arm, his shoulder still aching like crazy. "Is there any way to get the keys back?"

"That's reasonable. We'll go to the morgue, get his personal effects, and I'll drop you off at the campground," Casey offered. "Where's the other kid that was with you?"

"I don't know, sir. Doug disappeared right after ... Ty shot you. He said he didn't want to be part of any killing."

"Smart kid."

The three boys then scurried out the door and headed to the scout car before the sheriff changed his mind.

OOO

Casey thought it wise to not make a report on this incident. Tawny could very well have saved their lives—especially his—and he would not make her the subject of a manslaughter investigation. And hopefully those boys, having the shit kicked out of them by a girl, were humiliated enough to straighten up.

It was still early in the day so he headed to the Luna Landing for some gas and to check on how the station was doing, hoping they were still vandal free.

"Good morning, Sheriff," Colter greeted.

"I was going to ask for some gas, but without power, your pumps don't work, right?" Casey frowned once he realized his error.

"That's true, but I do have a small generator that I have wired for one pump and a fan for the store. Pull up to number three and we'll get you filled. Alex!" Colter called out. "How about taking care of the sheriff?"

Casey recognized Alex and grinned, following Colter into the minimart.

"You've got yourself a helper? Alex is a nice boy," Casey said.

"Yes, he is, and so are his brothers once you get to know them. Alex is helping out here while his brothers are collecting empty water bottles. Then Alex drives them over to the campground where they refill the bottles. I get half of them to give away here, and the boys are passing the rest out to the neighbors. All it has cost me so far is a couple gallons of gas and the boys not only stay out of trouble, but they are doing something good *and* keeping the other kids away from here—a win-win as far as I'm concerned."

"I wish there were more shop owners with your attitude," Casey confessed.

"So do I, Sheriff. As I see it, this lockdown is going to hurt us all. With it being during Kapac Days, it's going to be devastating to the livelihood of many shop owners and for the general economy of this town too. I know it's only been a week so far, but it's our busiest week of the year. There will be businesses that won't recover. I'm hoping Linden's survives after last night."

"What happened last night?" Casey asked, alarmed.

"A group from the campground broke in and ransacked the place. They busted up the front door really bad, too."

"What about Carl? Is he okay?"

"I haven't seen, Carl," Colter admitted, "but I do have the boys on the lookout for some plywood to seal up the door."

"I know where there is some. Meet me there in half an hour." Casey rushed out.

OOO

10:00 am

"Mom, do you think it would be okay if we went outside for a while? We could set up the croquet game or something. I'd rather play badminton, but I know it's too hot," Meg asked.

"I think that might be okay as long as you don't make too much noise. I'm concerned about drawing attention to us," Becca explained. She followed her daughter down to the basement where the other three teens were. Sandy was already sorting through the games closet.

"Justin, do you have any weapons training of any kind?" Becca asked painfully. She felt it odd she would be asking an almost total stranger to protect her children. "I can't recall Sandy ever shooting a gun."

"Yes, ma'am. I'm in ROTC at school and they have trained us in handguns and rifles in preparation for a possible military career," Justin answered respectfully.

"Do you plan on going into the Army after graduation?"

"I'm undecided at this point, ma'am, but I am considering it. May I ask why you want to know?" Justin questioned.

"If the four of you are going to be outside, it might be wise for someone to be on guard duty, and it looks like that might be you. Can you handle a shotgun? The sheriff left us two for protection," Becca said.

"Yes, ma'am, shotguns are easy: point and shoot." Justin grinned and squared his shoulders, pleased he had something to do that would repay Becca's kindness for taking him and Tawny in—although Tawny put a big dent in the debt they owe.

"I'll be right back." Becca hurried up the stairs and returned with one of the shotguns and a fist full of 12-gauge shells, handing them over to the young man.

Justin turned his back to the group, aiming the weapon at the floor while he checked the chamber. Seeing it was unloaded, he then slid the shells in and pocketed the rest.

"So what have you decided on playing?"

"Like I said, Mom, badminton or volleyball would be too strenuous in this heat, so I'm thinking of croquet, and if that's too boring or too hot, we can always come back inside and play cards or monopoly," Meg answered, dragging the croquet set to the glass door and out into the yard.

OOO

Casey drove his scout car while Frank followed in an old pickup truck to Linden's Grocery. Colter was already there waiting. Together, they unloaded four sheets of plywood and stacked it against the building.

"I'm going inside to see if I can find Carl," Casey announced. Grabbing his flashlight, he stepped into the dim light and the chaos. He headed for the back area, maneuvering around the overturned shelves and crunching crackers and dry cereal under his boots. Various sweet and sour odors mingled in the air and Casey took a breath through his mouth. He stepped in something squishy and ignored it.

Past the swinging doors, he stopped. "Carl? It's Sheriff WhiteCloud. Are you here?" Casey called out. He could hear footsteps overhead, and then coming from the wall. A near-invisible door swung open.

"I'm very happy to see you, Sheriff," Carl whispered.

"Are you okay, sir?"

"Oh, sure. Those vandals didn't know I was upstairs. I kept quiet until they all left." He walked out into the store. "Quite a mess, isn't it?"

"It sure is, Carl. Colter, Frank and I are here to board up the front door. And I'm assuming you have a back entrance?"

"Yes, there is another more secure door I can use." The elderly man looked around again and sighed. "I do appreciate what you and the others are doing for me. Thank you. I'm not going to worry about cleaning up this mess until everything is back to normal. Do you have any idea when that might be?"

"No, but after we take care of your door, I'm going to find out. Are you going to be okay here by yourself?"

"I'll be fine. There's nothing left for anyone to steal, so I doubt they'll be back."

"If there is anything you need, come and find me. I'll either be on rounds or I'll be at the Burns house at the back of the subdivision."

The three men wrestled with the plywood to cover the door and used the bed of Frank's pickup truck to reach the higher areas to nail the sheets of wood in place.

Colter had thought to bring a broom and swept up the glass on the outside, dumping it all into a bucket he always kept in his truck.

OOO

At precisely noon, the sheriff drove up to the barricade on the north side of town. Expecting to see the same group of soldiers from the day before, he was surprised when he didn't recognize any of them.

"I'm sorry, sir, the town is still in quarantine. Please turn around and go back home."

"Get it right, soldier. I'm the sheriff of this town, and I was told to come back here at this time to talk with Lt. Murphy. Now where is he?"

"I'm not familiar with a Lt. Murphy, Sheriff," the armed soldier said.

"Then get me whoever your commanding officer is and get him now!" Casey snarled. He was fed up with being run in circles.

A few minutes later, an officer approached the barrier, and like his predecessor, he stayed ten feet away, out of reach of any angry citizens. "I'm Major Ron Mesic. What can I do for you, Sheriff?"

"I was to talk with Lt. Murphy today about when the paperwork from the CDC would be ready and we would be released from this trumped-up lockdown."

"I have no idea who this Lt. Murphy is that you are referring to. Command was passed off to this squad early this morning and nothing was said about the quarantine being lifted any time soon," Major Mesic answered. "Is there anything else I can do for you, sir?"

"I've got teens committing suicide, adults trashing stores, and a serial killer loose. My town is falling apart! So, yeah, if we're not let out of here in the next 24 hours, you can get me another supply of body bags!" Casey turned on his heel and got back in his squad car. He punched the steering wheel in frustration and squealed his tires in anger as he left. He had visited one or the other of the barricades daily and never got a straight answer from anyone.

Casey cruised up and down each street for something to do. Memories of holding Becca last night haunted his thoughts and he smiled, his anger sliding away. This whole mess had only one bright side: it had brought him and Becca back together.

CHAPTER TWENTY-ONE

Noticing a crowd of adults gathered around an older man standing on a bench at the park, Casey stopped to listen. He leaned against his squad car, making his presence known, yet not making any move to disperse the crowd. Why should he? They really weren't doing anything wrong or illegal, at least not yet.

"This is God's punishment for our sins!" the preacher yelled, wiping the sweat from his forehead with a small towel. "First, He delivered a plague to our town, but being a merciful God, it was contained before any of us became ill. Then He took away the electricity—electricity which he allowed us to discover to make life easier for us, but we abused it!" The old man went on. "Electricity which powered those damnable phones and devices that have corrupted our youths!" The crowd murmured in agreement. "But that wasn't enough to get our attention, oh no. He had to take away even more, our food and water, which we cannot live without!

"And then the rains came and the heat, the impossible heat. He is warning us what Hell will be like if we continue on this path!

"Are we awake yet, my friends? Are we ready to leave behind our sinful ways and repent? Are we ready to ...?" a shot rang out and a red smear blossomed in the preacher's chest. He collapsed, falling backward off the bench while the frightened crowd ran panicked in multiple directions.

Casey ducked further behind his squad car, pulling his weapon. He turned and scanned behind him, the direction the shot came from. He could see nothing, no movement of any kind—no one running from the scene, not even a flutter of curtain from the subdivision behind the row of businesses where the shot originated. It was as if the shooter was never there.

Casey ran crouched to the preacher. He didn't need to check the pulse, as the blood pattern began at the heart. It appeared someone knew what they were doing and took the perfect killing shot. Casey went back to the protection of his car and called for the hearse, while still scanning the area for anything, *anything* out of the ordinary. All was quiet—too quiet.

A half-hour later, after Mr. Johnson left with yet another body, Casey continued driving around, watching, looking for anyone that didn't belong.

Turning up Spring Street, he noticed Josh's blue and white work van parked in front of the Bates house. He slowed to a stop as Josh walked out the front door carrying something, obviously preoccupied.

"Everything okay, Josh?" he asked.

Josh stopped, clenching and unclenching his fingers wrapped around the lead pipe in his hand. "No, it's not okay, and it's all *your* fault!" he said with a snarl.

"What are you talking about, Josh?" Casey remained outwardly calm although he noticed the pipe in Josh's hand had splotches of blood and there was more blood on his forearm. He casually leaned against the front bumper of his squad car, hoping to present a non-threatening posture yet remained alert.

"I was finally going to get my chance with her after all these years of patiently waiting, then you had to come along and ruin it!"

"Her? Her who, Josh?" Casey asked, cautiously standing up straighter.

"Becca, you ignorant half-breed! I've always loved her but now she wants only *you*," he half sobbed. "I'm really angry, Casey, mostly at her for rejecting me ... *again and again*, but I could never hurt her, never. My therapist said to take my anger out on something else. So I did. Only the relief didn't last. I had to hurt someone else, and then another. And it's *your* fault for getting in my way!" Josh screamed as he lunged at Casey, who easily side-stepped the attack.

Casey's jaw clenched and his nostrils flared at the racial slur. He knew instinctively this was not the time to address that and let it slide.

"Stop it, Josh! I don't want to hurt you, but I will not let you hurt anyone else." Then it dawned on him what Josh was saying. "You killed all those people, didn't you, either by cutting their throats or strangling them, right? Did you hit them in the head with that pipe first?" Casey stalled for time. Why he was stalling was a mystery to him—no backup would be coming. This was on him alone to deal with.

Josh glared at the sheriff.

"Yeah, I wanted to knock them out first so they wouldn't feel pain like I was feeling."

"Why those people, Josh? How did you decide who to kill?"

"It really was only because they were alone, like me." Josh sobbed and lunged again. Casey evaded him once again then Josh turned quickly and attacked again from a closer range. Casey went on the offensive instead of evading him once more and punched him. Josh dropped the lead pipe and went after the sheriff with both fists. Casey had years of military police training and experience with drunks and drugged-out crazies. Even with all his anger fueling him, Josh was no match for the lawman. Two more punches and Josh was face down on the ground with Casey's knee in his back. He pulled the metal handcuffs from his back pocket and had them in place before Josh realized what happened.

Getting Josh to his feet was more difficult than Casey anticipated with his arm not at full capacity. Josh was still fighting his capture as Casey opened the back door of the scout car and shoved his prisoner in. With Josh secure, Casey darted into the house.

"Mrs. Bates?" he called out. Not getting any answer, he began searching the rooms. Josh's other victims were posed in the kitchen and that's where he found Mrs. Bates, in a pool of blood. Josh had escalated again and had beaten her to death with that lead pipe. Bits of bone and brains along with wet blood were splashed across the table and on the cupboards, dripping down to the floor and spreading out forming puddles of dark red.

Casey waited until Mr. Johnson left with Mrs. Bates before taking Josh to the jail. After manhandling him into a cell, Casey locked the metal door and sat.

"If you calm down, Josh, I'll take the cuffs off."

"Okay, okay, then will you let me out of here?"

"The cuffs first, then we'll talk. Now see this slot? Turn around and put your hands in the slot." Casey made sure his weapon was secure and the strap was snapped tight. Then he pulled out the cuff key and released Josh's hands then he sat back down well out of reach of his prisoner's long arms.

"Just out of curiosity, how did you know that Becca and I had started seeing each other again?" he asked.

"I saw you two kissing out on the deck late the other night," Josh said.

"You were watching the house from the backyard? So you were stalking her."

"I wasn't stalking her, I was watching out for her, making sure she was safe. Can't you understand how I feel? How much I love her?"

"Actually, Josh, I can. You see, I love her too. The only difference is that she loves me back."

"But she could love me if it weren't for you!"

"Not after what you've done."

"She would never have known if I hadn't missed," Josh answered with a low growl.

"What do you mean?" Casey prodded.

"The preacher wasn't supposed to die," Josh looked at the sheriff from under hooded eyes, "but ... you moved."

Oxygen fled his brain as he focused on what Josh had said.

ooo

After leaving Josh a bottle of water, Casey left to find Becca. Outside, he paced beside his car, trying to come to terms with everything going on. How would he break this to her? She had known Josh for as long as she had known him and he was sure the news was going to be hard. The only way he knew for sure, was to be direct—gentle but direct. He headed home.

Casey struggled with the lockdown, the power outage, and the violence, just like everyone else. He might be the sheriff, but he was still a man, and he was still vulnerable like everyone else and his heart ached for the woman he loved.

"Becca?" he called out after entering the house.

"I'm in the kitchen," she answered.

"Come and sit down." He took her by the hand and sat her at the table. "There was a shooting in town. A man was preaching in the park. I didn't recognize him so I think he came from the campground. He wasn't doing any harm and I was going to let him be. Then a shot came from behind me. It was a long-range hit and I never saw the shooter. That preacher is now in the morgue."

Becca shivered. "Oh, how awful."

"As I was driving around looking for anyone suspicious or out of place, I found someone else. I caught the serial killer."

"What? That's great news! We are all safer now, right?"

"Yes, and when I caught him coming out of a house, he attacked me and I had to take him down. He's in a jail cell right now, and he confessed to the shooting too," Casey said, searching her face with his dark eyes.

"What are you not telling me?" Becca said, recognizing the tone in Casey's voice.

"The serial killer was aiming at *me* when he shot the preacher."

"What?! You're okay, right? Please tell me you're okay!" Becca whimpered, breathing fast and hard.

"I'm fine, but Becca ... the killer is Josh."

"That's not possible. Josh is one of the sweetest, shyest men in town!" Becca stood abruptly, backing away from Casey. "Why would he want to kill you?"

"I was in his way. Becca, sweetheart, Josh is a very, very angry man. He told me his therapist told him to take his anger and frustration out some way. I'm sure he didn't mean killing people, but that's what Josh started doing."

"But what did he have to be that angry about? Whenever I saw him, he always seemed happy," she protested.

Casey wiped his hands over his face and stood to face Becca. "He was angry that he couldn't have ... you."

"Me?" she questioned, and then the realization hit her. "Oh, dear God, he asked me out when he fixed the generator, and I said no, and then he brought us a jug of water and I told him we didn't need it. I rejected him twice and that's when the killing started, isn't it?" Becca frowned, her bottom lip quivered.

"This is NOT your fault, Becca. Josh is delusional, that's all, and with the stress of the lockdown, he snapped. As soon as possible, I will get him into the county jail and they likely will move him to a mental health facility where he can get some help." Casey pulled her into his arms to comfort her. She laid her cheek against his chest and listened to his heart beat and when she realized her heart was beating in the same rhythm, she knew Casey was right. She stepped back and smiled sadly at him.

"I know it's not my fault. Poor Josh." Completely changing the subject, she asked, "You hungry? Rita is grilling burgers for lunch."

"I'm always hungry." Casey smiled down at her and kissed her. "You're amazing, you know that?"

At that moment, Rita screamed.

They both rushed to the deck to find Rita sitting on a chair, rocking and holding her hand, crying.

"What happened?" Becca knelt in front of her.

"I felt a little woozy and reached out to steady myself and accidentally set my hand on the grill cover," she whimpered. "It really, really hurts, Becca. What are we going to do?"

"We just so happen to have a doctor in the house. Casey?" Becca looked at him and he left to find Micah. "Now let's get some cold water on that."

"Not butter?" Rita let herself be led into the kitchen.

"No, not butter, that's an old wives' tale! Cold water will stop the tissue from further damage and take the sting away." Becca ran the water until cold then turned the sprayer on gentle, putting Rita's hand under the heavy mist.

"That does feel better." Rita pulled her hand away and it immediately started to hurt again. She pushed her hand back under the sprayer and leaned on the sink.

"Rita, I want to tell you something before they come back." Becca smile coyly. "Last night, Casey asked me to marry him and I said yes."

"That is the best news of the day! So much for taking it slow, eh?" Rita hugged her friend and then quickly got her hand back under the cold water.

"What happened?" a very concerned Micah set his black bag on the table and went to the sink. He put his chest against Rita's back, encircling her with his arms and put both hands around her wet wrist to assess the damage. She sighed at the comforting gesture and Micah blushed. "Keep your hand under the water while I get some cream and bandages. Becca, I'll need a soft towel to dry her hand when the time comes," he said after examining the burn while water sluiced over both of them.

He dried her hand gently but quickly and then spread a white cream over the red lesions, which instantly took the pain away.

"What is that stuff?" Rita asked.

"Silvadene sulfadiazine—the best burn cream I've come across." Micah then wrapped her hand with wide gauze and secured it with a small piece of tape. "I'm going to change the dressing every hour, so don't go anywhere," he said, smiling at her.

"What? You're not going to kiss it to make it better?" Rita teased, her lips fighting to smile in spite of her pain.

Micah broke into a boyish grin, and while gazing into her dark gray eyes, picked up her hand and kissed each fingertip of the burned hand. Warmth spread through his core, outward and everywhere as he blushed.

Rita swallowed hard as she watched the erotic gesture. Becca grinned, watching Rita turn several shades of red.

Micah packed up the ointment and gauze into his black bag and took it back downstairs.

"What's up with you and Micah?" Becca blurted out as soon as the doctor was out of hearing range.

"I sorta made a pass at him a few days ago that he rejected," Rita confessed. "I think he's changed his mind."

CHAPTER TWENTY-TWO

Sandy was bumped out of the croquet game early and found a spot in the shade next to Justin, yet kept his focus on the girls.

"I have noticed the way you look at my sister," Sandy said, eyes still forward.

"Yeah? And I've noticed how you look at *my* sister." Justin bumped his shoulder against Sandy. "I've got a proposition for you: I'll let you date my sister if you let me date yours. How's that? I know you're concerned about Meg's safety, but don't be, please. Tawny would tear me limb from limb if I hurt Meg in any way."

Sandy glanced at his friend. *Yes,* he thought, *Justin had become his friend, perhaps even his best friend over the last two weeks.* "You know, this might not be up to us, Justin. *They* have the final say." Sandy tilted his head toward the girls who were now giggling over something.

"Ah, yes, but I happen to know that Tawny really likes you, and if you asked her to the homecoming dance, she would say yes. Tell you what—why don't we double date?" Justin offered.

"Deal! And if I tell Meg she can go to the dance with a date as long as the date is you, she wouldn't hesitate."

Justin playfully splayed his hand on his chest. "Oh, you crush me, Sandy, and question my appeal to your little sister, who by the way, I think is beautiful and smart and funny. Okay, I tell you what, I'll ask Meg first, just to prove to you she likes me ... maybe to prove to myself that she would say yes before you tell her she can."

"Hi, Meg!" a new voice called out.

Justin stood and racked a cartridge into the shotgun, a very distinct and unnerving sound.

"Stop right where you are," Justin said coldly.

Alex went still and held his hands out to the side. In each hand was a bottle of water. He turned slowly toward the unfamiliar young man holding the shotgun pointed at him and one of his younger brothers.

"You're not going to kill us, are you?" the younger boy cried.

"Shut up, Bobby. He's not going to kill us. Sit down where you are and *don't move!*" Alex warned his brother. "Sandy, could you please ask your friend to lower that weapon? We've come only to see if you need any water," Alex explained.

"Why would you be doing that?" Justin asked, still holding the shotgun level.

Alex straightened his shoulders. "We've been working with Mr. Colter in getting water to anyone who needs it."

"Who's this Mr. Colter?" Justin asked Sandy, not taking his eyes off the intruders.

"Colter owns the Luna Landing mini-mart and gas station. He's a good guy, and actually Justin, Alex is a good guy too. You can lower the gun," Sandy said.

Meg and Tawny joined their brothers under the shade of the tree, curious over what all the commotion was.

"If we're intruding, we'll leave," Alex offered. "Do you need this water or not? I'm sure I can find someone who does."

"We really don't, Alex, but that's nice of you to be doing that," Meg said. "Where are you getting bottled water?"

"My brothers are collecting the empties, and then I take them over to the campground and fill them there. Mr. Colter gets half to give away at the mart, and we take the rest around the subdivision. I know that's not the most sanitary method, but right now, no one cares."

"What's in it for you?" Justin asked, still leery.

"Colter gives me gas for the Camaro, and it keeps us busy. It gets pretty darn boring otherwise," Alex admitted.

Justin lowered the shotgun. "You have a Camaro?" he asked in awe.

"Yeah, a 1968, in sea-mist green. I rebuilt it myself."

"What size engine?"

"427, auto with a console shift."

"I bet that really moves," Justin said. "Can I see it sometime?"

"Sure, it's parked out front." Justin and Alex started up the hill, talking cars.

"Hold on a second, Justin," Sandy said. "Remember what Casey said about us staying together. I'll be right with you." Justin nodded and shifted the shotgun to a more comfortable position while they waited, continuing their conversation about engines.

Sandy helped retrieve the croquet mallets and then ushered the two girls back into the house so he could join Justin and Alex on the grassy slope to go see the car, much to the chagrin of the girls. Meg and Tawny weren't interested in the car, but a different face was appealing. However, Meg knew Alex and knew his entire focus would be on that car of his.

CHAPTER TWENTY-THREE

August 15
Tuesday
6:00 pm

"Micah, I feel silly asking for an escort, but would you come with me while I collect a few things from my house?" Rita asked the doctor. "I feel like I've got a wounded wing!"

He smiled at her. "It would be my pleasure, Rita. As comfortable as this place is, I'm getting a first-hand taste of cabin fever! Like most, I'm accustomed to being active. This sitting around is boring, even if I do learn from the medical journals I brought along."

As they strolled down the driveway and across the street, Micah asked casual questions.

"So you've lived in Kapac your entire life?"

"For the most part, yeah. I did leave for a year when I went to Ohio Tech to learn more about computers," Rita answered.

"It's such a small town, I'm surprised you can earn a living here."

She laughed. "The world wide web makes it easy. Besides, I paid cash for my house after my mother died, so my expenses are really low." Rita found herself giving more personal information to him than she normally would, but she also noted he was easy to talk to, and she tended to forget he was her doctor.

"And what about you, Micah? You're a handsome man in a lucrative profession ... why aren't you married with a couple of kids?"

He smiled down at her, enjoying her bluntness, and replied, "Guess I haven't found the one person I wanted to settle down with. And why aren't you married?"

"Same reason, I guess," she answered, unlocking her door.

Micah wandered around her house, getting a feel for the woman behind the computer, while Rita collected things from her office, stuffing them in her oversized purse. The purse was getting full since she now always kept her laptop and files with her. She turned to leave the room and found Micah standing in the doorway watching her. She moved toward him, expecting him to move out of her way—instead, he reached for her.

"Oh, I know this is wrong in so many ways and I may regret it, but I've wanted to do this for months." Micah cupped her face and slid his long fingers into her short black hair, pulling her close and kissing her.

When he released her, Rita smiled and asked, "Now why would you regret that? Remember, you're entitled to a life too. And as much as I liked that—really, really liked that—maybe it's not a good idea ... I don't want to put you in danger, Micah."

He looked at her with questioning eyes.

"Someone is either trying to really scare me and hurt me or wants me dead," she said bluntly, her jaw clenched tightly.

"I know," Micah answered with a sigh. "And they sent me."

"Explain that," Rita said tightly. She straightened her body and jerked away, backing further into her office, putting some distance between them.

"There's a government agency I owe a debt to, a promise I made many years ago to do one thing, anything they told me to do. They called in their marker. Apparently, you have stepped on some toes, and they want you eliminated."

"Was all of this, all of what's going on, set up just to get to *me*?" She said nothing else, but he saw her eyes fill with tears. "It doesn't make sense. Why would someone, some agency, hurt so many people just to hurt me? I'm nobody."

"I don't know, but it wouldn't surprise me—they can be ruthless. And you're *not* a nobody. You're smart and you're dangerous to them. And maybe they're doing it because ... they can. I want you to know that I can't do it, Rita. I can't kill you! I think I fell in love with you the first time you walked into my office. You're so smart, brilliant at what you do, and you're funny and kind and beautiful. I was crushed when I found out you were the target."

"How are you going to do it?" she said with a calm that surprised him.

"The easiest and least painful would be to overdose your insulin."

"Have you already been manipulating my meds?" She caught him in a dark gaze.

"Yes." He turned his head slightly in embarrassment and shame.

"I don't want Becca to find ... me," Rita said, lifting her chin in defiance.

"You haven't been listening, Rita," Micah said, agitated. "I can't do it! I can't ... kill you!"

"If you don't, whoever this is will just send someone else."

"I know." He bowed his head in defeat.

"I don't want to die, Micah. Can you fake my death somehow? And then I can just disappear," she pleaded.

"Before we talk about that, will you spend one night with me?" he asked shyly. "We need to go to the clinic first and I'll re-calibrate your insulin pump so you can start using it again while we try to figure something out."

"I thought you sent my pump back to the manufacturer," Rita questioned, tilting her head in confusion.

"There's nothing wrong with your pump, so it's still on my desk. I just wanted to get you back on injections," Micah confessed.

"I see." Rita searched his face for a moment and saw only hurt and honesty. "Okay, as selfish as it might sound, I'd like to *know* you before I die," she confessed with a mischievous lusty grin. "I'll text Becca and let her know we won't be back for a while, or else she'll wait up until dawn." Rita sighed, hopeful for something other than death.

OOO

As evening approached, John and Margi Maguire collected the solar lanterns that had been recharging all day on the picnic table just outside of the Kapac House Bed & Breakfast.

Breakfast that morning had been canned Vienna sausages, canned corned beef hash, and the last box of crackers, distributed evenly among the fourteen of them. Not the usual nourishing fare they were accustomed to feeding their guests, but at least no one went without something to eat.

"It saddens me to say we are now out of food." Margi looked at each of the twelve guests with sincere regret. "You are all welcome to continue to stay here until the power comes back on, but we can't feed you any longer."

"At least here we have shelter from these weird thunderstorms," one of the regular guests said, picking up their lantern and retiring to their second-floor room. The other five couples followed suit and soon the proprietors were left alone at the massive antique dining table that hadn't been moved in almost a hundred years.

"I'm glad we've decided to reduce our availability to guests," John said to his wife of fifty years. "This has been a tremendous strain on both of us." Margi nodded, noticing how gaunt John was starting to look. He took one full oil lamp and set it safely in the center of the big dining room table as a night light, while Margi took the other one to their private quarters.

With all of the rooms being sound-proofed during the last remodeling, the noise of the strong winds and thunder were muted, allowing the guests to sleep deeply. With a particularly loud crash of lightning and thunder, a heavy branch broke through a window, unheard, and landed on the table, tipping over the oil lamp.

The kerosene oozed across the highly polished wood, soaking the lacy cloth placemats, and the flame from the wick ignited the fuel. Fire dripped from the table edge and set the old area rug underneath ablaze. With the wind coming through the window to fan the flames, the fire spread quickly, and the old house went up like the 100-year-old tinderbox it was—the old dry timbers were fully engulfed in minutes.

Without power, the smoke alarms remained silent. John had changed the battery in the one alarm not on the grid yet in his haste, he put the battery in backward, making it non-functioning. Without power, there was no alerting the fire department, even if there was someone to take the call. Without people on the street enjoying Kapac Days festivities to sound an alarm, fourteen people perished in the fire.

ooo

Rita and Micah emerged from the physician's lounge flushed and glowing from an evening of passion.

"I can't let you go, Rita. I'm 48 years old and I feel like a teenager with his first crush." Micah gave her a long firm but gentle hug, being very careful with her burned hand. His attention was then pulled to the lobby.

The glow from the fire further down the beach lit up the emergency entrance of the dark clinic. Micah grabbed Rita's good hand and they ran toward the fire, only to be stopped a hundred yards away by the intense heat. Smoke hung low to the ground like a fog creeping in from the water, swirling as the flames pulsed. The fire was burning out almost as quickly as it started, leaving behind the beginnings of a charred ruin.

"Oh, my God, no one could survive that blaze!" Micah lamented. "I pray no one was inside. What was that building?" The excessive heat from the blaze forced them to retreat further and further away.

"It was the Kapac House Bed & Breakfast and the oldest building in town. They were always full during the summer." Rita swallowed a sob, and then her eyes went wide when she saw only a few people watching the fire from the other side. "I have an idea. Come on!"

They made their way back to the clinic and in the cloak of darkness, Rita pulled out her phone and sent Becca another text:

> Micah and I had a tiff. I'm spending the night at the B&B. See you in the morning.

She hit send and turned to Micah, wide-eyed. "I just died."

CHAPTER TWENTY-FOUR

August 16
Wednesday

At 3:00 am, the pounding on the front door woke Casey and Becca.

A very distraught Dr. Micah Jones stood under the porch light, clutching the door frame, his head hanging low.

"Micah, what is it? Come in." Becca opened the door wide as he stumbled in. "Where's Rita?"

"I gather she's not here. We were together for a while at the clinic, and then we had a fight, a small misunderstanding really, and she stomped out." He swallowed hard, trying to remember what they had discussed as a simple cover story. "And now I can't find her."

"Let me call her," Becca said, turning her phone on. "Ah, there's a text from her." Becca opened the mail, read it, and said, "She's fine. She's spending the night at the B&B. I'll go there and pick her up in the morning."

"The ... Kapac House?" Micah sobbed. "It just burned to the ground."

Shocked, Becca burst into tears. "No," she choked out and collapsed.

ⵔⵔⵔ

After getting Becca back into bed with a sedative, the two men drove back to the scene of the fire. Casey pulled out a roll of crime scene tape from his trunk and began blocking off access to the charred building. His heart was heavy with grief for Becca, for Rita, for the doctor who was now his friend, for the whole town. His feet felt like lead as he walked around the once-grand building, feeding out the yellow plastic tape that might or might not keep others safe. Back to the starting point, he fell to his knees, staining his pressed pants in the singed grass and ashes, and wept.

The sheriff stood, now angry over the loss, and got into his car and headed out to the barricade. In a blind rage, he made it all the way to Walstroms before he realized the barricade was gone. On returning to his town, he also noticed the street lights were coming on. Power had been restored.

He stopped at the clinic to find Micah still guiding himself through the rooms with a flashlight.

"Micah," Casey called out and flipped a light switch on. The room lit up, startling the doctor.

"Lights are good," Micah stated, his voice heavy with a forced sadness.

"The barricades are gone too."

"Even better." He looked around the once sterile room and then back at the sheriff. "I'm sorry, Casey, I can't stay here. Without Rita, I'm empty. If the road is open, I'm going home ... eventually all the way home, back to Chicago." He held out his hand and Casey shook it. "Please tell Becca thank you for all she's done for me, for Rita," his voice caught with a sob, "for everyone. And if I can leave you with one piece of advice, Sheriff, *marry* that woman!"

"I intend to," Casey replied.

As the doctor lingered beside his car after tossing his overnight bag into back seat, the sheriff got into his and headed home.

OOO

9:00 am

"This means we can go home, Tawny," Justin said to his twin sister. He turned to Sandy. "Can you give us a lift back to the church camp? My car is still parked there and I'll take us home. My mom will be really glad to see us. Ms. Burns, thank you so very much for allowing us to stay with you. It's a debt I doubt we will ever be able to repay." Becca, still subdued with intense grief, hugged both teens goodbye.

At the campground parking lot, Justin opened the hatch to his compact car, and they tossed their duffle bags inside. Tawny moved first, putting her arms around Sandy's neck and kissing him, molding her body to his.

Justin moved to Meg and smiled. "Don't forget, we have a date for homecoming. Two in fact: yours and ours." Then he ran his fingers gently down Meg's cheek and lifting her chin with a finger, kissed her gently and pulled her close to his body.

OOO

Throughout the day, as the population of Kapac became aware of having the power restored and more so that they were no longer captive in the town, they moved about, reopening stores and picking up the pieces of their lives—lives that for the most part were forever changed.

The Kapac House stood like a giant skeleton with the metal plumbing and the brick fireplaces the only visible reminder of the grandeur that once was. Smoke tainted the air, sending the smell across the water on a clean and cooling breeze.

Those that were locked *out* of the town began returning a few at a time. As word spread, more and more happily took up residence in their homes again.

With no barricades to stop him, David Burns drove straight to the back of the subdivision to the house he had shared with Becca and their children. He pounded on the door until someone opened it.

Casey glowered at David. "What do you want, David? And you better make it quick before I arrest you for violating your restraining order."

"How are my kids? I want to see them," he asked, shocked to see the sheriff at his house.

"Sandy and Meg are fine, Becca is fine, Rita is dead. And … Lisa is dead. Now leave."

David stood, too shocked by the news to move.

"Dad?" Both Sandy and Meg had come silently up behind Casey when they heard their father's voice.

"Oh, Meg, Sandy, it's so good to see you! Are you okay? This must have been very hard on you both." When David opened his arms to them, they didn't approach him. He looked confused, then hurt, then angry, all in a matter of seconds.

"It wasn't all that hard, Dad," Sandy said. "Mom took very good care of us and several others."

"We also learned a lot, Dad … about you. How could you have *lied* to us about mom having an affair when it was really *you*? And we know now about your other wife and your girlfriend, who committed suicide because of you." Meg's anger poured out of her. "Quite frankly, Dad, I have a lot to think about and I don't want to see you for a while." And she backed away.

"Don't call us, we'll call you." Sandy put his arm protectively around his sister and led her to the kitchen.

David was angry. "What lies have you been poisoning them with?"

Becca came up behind Casey. "Only the truth, David, only the truth—something that seems to evade you. Tomorrow we bury over three dozen people, including my best friend of almost thirty years." The tears ran down her face anew. "That list also includes your girlfriend and your unborn child. Now, get out of here, David!" Becca shouted, the tears leaking from her already red eyes as she turned and walked out of the room.

"You better leave now, David." Casey held the door open in an obvious and deliberate hint.

OOO

"That was an incredible show of maturity on your part, both of you. I'm very proud of you." Becca hugged her children. "I'm going to wash my face, and then we have something to discuss with you."

After Becca left the room, Casey ushered Becca's children into the kitchen.

Casey chuckled. "This seems to be the best place to talk. Your mom has made it a warm and welcoming room." He poured himself a glass of water and sat. "Geesh, I never thought I would be nervous talking to teens about their mother—usually it's the other way around." He took a sip.

"Can we make this easier on you, Sheriff? We know you really like our mom and she likes you too," Sandy said. "Are you going to ask us if you can date her?"

Becca laughed from the doorway. "I told you this would be easier than you thought."

Casey smiled at her as she took her seat beside him.

"I promise to be better to her than David was, and to the two of you. I will never lie to you either." Casey paused. "You might not have known that your mother and I dated in high school but that ended when she went off to college, met and married your father. We've stayed friends and being a friend is a good way to build a solid relationship." He looked at Sandy and Meg and smiled, taking Becca's hand.

"Casey asked me to marry him, and I said yes," Becca finished.

There was only a moment of shocked silence until Sandy and Meg jumped out of their respective seats and hugged Becca and then Casey.

"Wow, oh wow!" Meg was all smiles. "When is the wedding? Can I be your bridesmaid? I can't wait to tell Tawny!"

ONE WEEK LATER

James Montro knocked gently on Becca's front door, his fingers nervously clenching and unclenching around the handle of his leather briefcase. There wasn't much inside, only a few papers, but he knew he needed to get this over with.

"Sheriff?" James said, startled to see Casey there. "I need to speak with Becca, is she here?"

"Come on in, Jim. Can I ask what this is about?"

"I have some ... legal papers to go over with her."

Becca walked in from the kitchen on hearing the familiar voice. "Mr. Montro? Is this about David?"

"No, Becca, it's about Rita," he said softly. "Can we sit somewhere?"

Casey put his arm around Becca and led her back to the kitchen with Jim following. After sitting, the lawyer opened his briefcase, removed the few papers, and pushed the case aside.

He took a deep breath and said, "I am so very sorry for your loss, Becca. Rita was a wonderful person and we are all going to miss her." He took a sip of water that Casey had set down in front of him before continuing. "I will try to keep this as brief as possible. Rita came to me several months ago to update her will. I know you're well aware Rita has ... had no living relatives and that she loved you like a sister.

"Rita Martin left everything to you, Rebecca: her house, car, bank accounts, and her life insurance policy. Everything, including this letter, with instructions I was to give this to you after she died. Please understand she felt her death would come as a result of her diabetic condition, *not* how it did."

Tears welled up in Becca's eyes, and Casey handed her a clean handkerchief. She smiled sadly at him; he'd been giving her his handkerchiefs all week, a never-ending supply it seemed.

"She did have some stipulations regarding the house: sell it and everything in it. She felt the contents would be best to donate to the charity of your choice or leave with the house when it sold. She didn't want you to keep anything that would make you sad." Jim paused to take another sip of water, trying to hide his own grief. "I took the liberty of closing her bank accounts, per her instructions—here is the check. And another check for the life insurance." He laid both on the table in front of her. "I just need a signature at your name, stating that you have received the funds."

Becca took the offered pen and signed her name, not looking at the checks.

"You liked Rita," Becca stated, not asked.

"Yes, I did. She was a wonderful person. Her death was a true tragedy." James Montro stood and reached into his pocket, extracting a set of keys. "These are to the house and her car, which I believe is still parked at the clinic."

As he started to leave, Becca came up to him and said, "Thank you for being her friend, Jim." And she hugged him before he walked out the door.

Jim stopped. "Oh, I almost forgot. The day after the power went out here, I received an anonymous email at my home in Dresden, leading me to a bank account David failed to disclose in the divorce. The court saw the wisdom in seizing it and you should start to get regular child support payments, plus the back child support, until those funds are depleted.

David should know that he can run but he can't hide from his responsibilities."

○○○

"Becca, you really should look at this," Casey said. Becca leaned over his shoulder and stared at the checks that totaled a half million dollars.

Becca sniffled. "I'd rather have Rita."

Casey held her close. "Are you going to read her letter?"

She moved back to the table where the envelope lay and picked it up. She fingered the flap for a moment and then carefully opened it.

Dear Becca,

I'm so sorry you are reading this because it means I'm dead. That's very surreal to me to say that because at the moment I'm quite alive.

Where do I even begin?

You've been the best friend I could ever have hoped for, and more than the sister I never had. You never questioned me when I didn't want to tell you something and I appreciated that, mainly because I didn't want to explain it was for your own safety that you didn't know. And I still can't say any more than that.

I know that if you have this letter, Jim Montro has already taken care of my will and my wishes. I know too that the amount I'm leaving you is a shock. The computer business can be quite lucrative and I have had little to spend it on except for retiring someday—that's now yours. Don't you dare try to give it away! You need it to take care of those beautiful kids of yours.

And unless I died in an accident and my car is totaled, I would like you to give it to Sanders as my thank you for mowing my lawn all the time, without even asking and without pay. Some tip, eh? And please give something appropriate to Omega—from me. I would ask you to not grieve for me, but I know that would be an impossible request, so I ask that you not grieve too long.

Finally, please find some happiness, you not only deserve it, you've earned it.

I love you my friend,
Rita

OOO

The following day, Alex Thornton called Becca and asked her to come to his office, at her convenience. He greeted her with a sincere hug.

"I'm so sorry for your loss, Becca," he said.

"Thank you, Alex," she said. "What is it you wanted to see me about?"

The attorney eyed Casey for a moment. "Please have a seat. I have something from your aunt. She asked me to give you this six weeks after your divorce from David." He slid a 9x6 yellow envelope across the desk to her.

"She was that certain that I would divorce David?"

"Yes, she was."

"Do you know what is in here?" Becca asked quietly.

"No, I do not. All she gave me were verbal instructions. Whatever is in there, she said you would know what she's trying to tell you." Alex leaned back in his chair, watching Becca's face and keeping a candid eye on Casey.

Becca gently opened the seal on the envelope and pulled out a picture: her prom picture. It was identical to the one Casey had on his desk. Her lip quivered as she smiled. "I wondered where this had gone to."

"May I see it?" Alex asked.

She nodded and handed it to him. His lips broke into a wide grin. "Your aunt's wisdom will never cease to amaze me." He turned to Casey. "May I ask what your intentions are regarding Rebecca?"

"My intentions? Not that it's any of your business, but I've already asked her to marry me," Casey said, slightly affronted.

"Ah, but it is my business." He turned to Becca again. "Elaine left you one more gift." He handed her another envelope and handed Casey the prom picture. "You see, Sheriff, apparently Becca's Aunt Elaine knew you were the one for her niece. That you would love her and treat her well."

Casey looked down at their prom picture and chuckled.

Becca opened the other, much larger envelope to discover the deed to her house.

TWO WEEKS LATER

"This is John Tasen, WROL, coming to you from Kapac, a town that has been through nearly two weeks of hell, and we still don't know why.

"Here with me today is Under Sheriff Casey WhiteCloud, Rebecca Burns, her two children, Sanders and Omega, Dr. Micah Jones, Mr. Joseph Johnson—the township coroner—Jonah Clews, Frank DeAngelo, both residents of Kapac, and the mayor Henry Hughes.

"Thank you all for agreeing to this interview. For the record, me and my cameraman have been here during this entire ordeal, with little contact with the TV station in the beginning and then none at all.

"So, what can you tell me and the viewing audience, about what was going on? Mr. Mayor?" John Tasen pointed the microphone in the mayor's direction.

"Quite honestly, I haven't a clue. My entire staff and I were out of town at a last-minute conference when the town was locked down and we couldn't get back in. No one ever contacted me for a statement and when I tried to call the sheriff, the phone lines were down. I had one conversation with an army fellow when I tried to go home but he wouldn't let me pass and told me things were *being handled.*"

"What about your statement about calling off Kapac Days?" the reporter asked.

"That wasn't me," the mayor stated.

John Tasen looked perplexed, and then turned his attention to Casey.

"Sheriff WhiteCloud, you were here the entire time. I spoke with you briefly when the spill first happened and a few times after that. What more can you tell me?"

Casey looked uncomfortable, and then seemed to make up his mind. He passed his hand over his face and said, "I was one of the first on the scene, John. Someone made a 911 call and that got the ball rolling. By the way, we found a disposable phone almost two miles closer to town, off on the roadside about a hundred feet in; it was new and the number matched the 911 call. The phone had been wiped clean so we weren't able to lift any prints. A delivery van was in an accident and spilled its contents. The state police were there first and I was next. However, within hours, *hours*, the military was there and both ends of town were locked down. It was as if they were in the wings, waiting. This all happened Sunday into Monday.

"People got agitated really fast when they couldn't get out, and then they realized there wasn't enough food to go around, and when the power went out Thursday during the night, all hell broke loose." Casey leaned back like he was finished. "And then the weather got strange: hot, humid, and the rain started."

"My friend ... thought the weather was being manipulated. It just kept getting hotter and hotter and more humid with the weird thunderstorms, and without power, there was no air conditioning," Becca said, swallowing her grief. "Not unless you had a generator, and even then, fuel was limited."

"With the power out, there wasn't any water and the sanitation quit," Casey added. "But we do live on a lake, and the resourceful ones took advantage of that. Even so, this quiet little town full of nice people turned on itself. There was rioting, looting and ... murder. And I will not go into those details since it's an active investigation."

"I witnessed the fire on the main street—a rather large house burnt to the ground. Any idea on what happened there? And why didn't the fire department show up?" John continued to the keep conversation flowing, even though he knew the answers.

"That's another of the odd co-incidences, just like my staff all being out of town. The fire trucks were all in Appleton being serviced and cleaned for the Kapac Days parade. And after talking with the firefighters, there was an apparent miscommunication that sent them all to Appleton at the same time, something that normally would not have been allowed," Mayor Hughes said.

"It was the Kapac House," Dr. Jones finally spoke up, his voice cracked with emotion. "A bed and breakfast that burned down. I was at the clinic a few doors down when I noticed the flames. It went up fast, so fast." He had agreed to return to Kapac for the interview and Rita's memorial.

"Tragic. Do you know how many lives were lost?" John prodded.

"We believe fifteen, but the fire burned so hot, there isn't much left," Casey said. Becca let out a sob and bolted from the room. Casey followed her.

"My mom's best friend was staying there," Meg whimpered and the tears flowed. "We all loved Rita." Sandy put his arm around his sister and held her while she cried.

OOO

When Becca and Casey returned to their seats, John Tasen picked up the microphone again.

"Was there anything else you noticed that seemed off to you?"

"In thinking back," Casey said and paused, "I went to the barricade daily, sometimes twice a day, and not once did any of the soldiers wear a mask or protective gear. In an area that was supposedly so contagious they had to isolate an entire town, I think that's rather odd. And the fogging that was supposed to take place to rid the town of some kind of virus never happened. We were told to stay indoors—indoors, in the blistering heat, without so much as a fan."

"Sheriff, looking back, is there anything you could've done differently that would have made it easier on the town?" he asked.

Casey snapped his head up and glared at the interviewer.

"Now you just wait a minute, buddy!" Frank DeAngelo said, rising from his seat. "Casey did more to keep this town together than you will ever know, including almost getting killed! He kept the peace as only one man can do when faced with the odds of a town filled with angry and scared people. He also got some of us together to board up Linden's grocery store and other businesses after they got busted into."

"And when we had a serial killer running around murdering people, Casey warned us, and then he found out who it was and took care of the situation! Don't you dare try to lay any of this on him!" Jonah Clews added, getting to his feet.

"I meant no disrespect," John apologized. He looked at the group in front of him and realized there was still one person that had remained silent. "Mr. Johnson, I understand you own and operate the funeral home in town, and you also have the position of the part-time coroner. Do you have anything to add?"

"Only that it might be time for me to retire," he answered slowly and sadly in his deep voice. "I'm quite accustomed to death, it's my job, but to see so many at one time, and for different causes, has taxed my resolve. And it hasn't really been about the death of the people, but perhaps the death of the town. The violence that I witnessed was unspeakable, and the violence of the young people was exceptionally hard. It's been as if they have no conscious, no sense of right or wrong, and for that I blame the parents." He stood. "Excuse me." With that, he left the house.

"Ms. Burns, thank you for letting me use your living room for this discussion." John Tasen turned off his mic and had Harry turn off the camera. He turned back to those still seated. "So, off the record: do any of you think that the weather was being manipulated to keep everyone indoors and subdued? That this was intentional and orchestrated?"

"Absolutely, but you'll never prove it."

EPILOGUE

Along a corridor of the inner halls of the Pentagon, Major Ron Mesic and Lieutenant Elias Murphy walked up to an unmarked door. Major Mesic turned the doorknob and stepped in, Murphy right behind him.

The name plate of the man seated at the metal desk merely said 'Secretary.' "Go right in, she's expecting you." The wooden door behind the secretary was bare of identification. The major once again entered first.

Cynthia Thompson smiled and leaned back in her chair. "You have a report for me?"

"Yes, ma'am," Lt. Murphy replied.

"What was the collateral damage?" she asked.

From memory, Mesic said, "Forty-three dead total—two by suicide, fifteen in a house fire, some by natural means, some not." As agreed, there was no paperwork that would leave a trail. "There was a house-to-house sweep after we left and more bodies were found. Those deaths were ruled natural from the heat. Oh ... and a dog."

"A dog?" Cynthia asked, alarmed. She had a fondness for animals.

"The dog had lapped up the blood from his murdered master. It was best to terminate the animal," Mesic continued. "Once an animal gets a taste of human blood or flesh, the animal becomes ... unpredictable."

"I see," Cynthia commented. "And the target?"

"She was in the house fire. This was after the asset gave her an overdose of insulin and left her there for someone else to find her body, to protect his cover story." The lack of emotion was mentally noted by the lieutenant.

"And our asset?"

"As soon as the lockdown ended, he disappeared per agreement, his obligation fulfilled."

"Excellent!" Cynthia sat forward in her leather chair. "Now, whose idea was it to bring in the trailer full of bottled water?"

"That was my doing, ma'am," Lt. Murphy confessed.

"And your reasoning?"

"It was part of the rule of three: you can live three weeks without food, three days without water, and three minutes without air. Once we shut the town down, taking away the access to food, we began the count of the three weeks. Next was to take away the power grid, which was easy enough to shut down. As I understood our mission, it was to terminate the target, not the entire town. On that third day without water, the people would begin to suffer from dehydration and we wanted them compliant, not dead. Simple: give them something they needed—water—to keep their thoughts away from what else we were taking, namely communications. They were then blind with no visual outside news. They were speechless without their phones, and they were deaf to all but what we wanted them to hear."

"How did you shut down the power?" Cynthia prodded.

"That was the easiest to do: we staged the spill to have the transformer inside the containment field where the power company couldn't access it. One of our technicians turned it off, and then turned it back on as we were leaving."

"Impressive. I'm curious ... how did you manage to get all the town key personnel out of the way on time?" she asked.

"That's where our other two assets came in, the two drivers," the major began the explanation. "One of them had been in position for two months, fitting into the town and volunteering as a fireman. That gave him access to the fire hall and consequently, the chief's computer. He sent out legitimate-appearing individual emails instructing each of the volunteers to be in Appleton at a certain time, which was before the lockdown. No one realized all key people were outside the containment area until it was too late.

"Then the assets blended back in at the campground to keep things stirred up. Those two did not know who the other asset was nor who the target was, and the main asset believed he was working alone."

"And how did you manage the communications issue?" she asked, already knowing the answer.

"The two at the campground were the ones with the dampening device to create the saturation test for a dense environment, taking out cell phone and internet for all except the very outlying areas of town. The device was built into the camper they used and completely shielded from detection. They turned it off from 2:00 am to 3:00 am to report in. During that brief time, anyone who was awake, which was unlikely, would have had cell coverage if they had a means to charge their phones, which was even more unlikely. We've done these tests before, for limited duration, and this was an excellent opportunity to test it for a long-term event," Mesic continued.

"You have both done very well. So what did we learn from this experiment?"

"That people can get really violent when you take away their comforts and their freedom. They were easily manipulated, ma'am. I found that … interesting," Lt. Murphey replied.

Cynthia grinned. These two were being trained and honed for something much bigger. "We will have a similar situation in a few months, except it will be during the dead of winter," she said stoically. "I'll be in touch. Dismissed."

OOO

A petite woman sat on a hard wooden bench in the balcony of the church, watching the funeral below. The big sunglasses and blonde wig hid her black hair and her identity. She really hated causing Becca such pain and grief, but it was safer for them both if Becca truly believed she had died in that fire.

Micah Jones stood behind her silently while she watched Becca cry. "I feel like Tom Sawyer," she said sadly.

"Are you ready to go?" he whispered in her ear.

She nodded, and after double-checking that her sleek computer and all the saved files were secure in her big purse, along with her various passports and off-shore bank books, she stood and they left by a side door.

The End

ACKNOWLEDGMENTS

I'd like to thank Rita Martin and Cynthia Thompson, for allowing me to use their names. These are two wonderful, kind, and longtime personal friends of mine, who are nothing like the characters the story portrays them as.

And many thanks to my beta readers for their insights and patience: my friend Sherry, my brother Tom, and my son Eric, a twenty-two-year military veteran. You are all very special to me and I love you.

And one last shout out to the art department at Permuted. The covers you do for me are always fabulous!

ABOUT THE AUTHOR

Deborah Moore is single and lives a quiet life in the Upper Peninsula of Michigan. She moved to the woods near a small town to pursue her dreams of being self-sufficient and to explore her love of writing.

Made in the USA
Las Vegas, NV
20 November 2020